Lionclaw

Lionclaw

A Tale of Rowan Hood

Nancy Springer

Philomel Books

New York

Philomel Books, a division of Penguin Putnam Books for Young Readers,
345 Hudson Street, New York, NY 10014. Philomel Books, Reg. U.S. Pat. & Tm. Off.
Published simultaneously in Canada. Printed in the United States of America.
Book design by Gunta Alexander. The text is set in Apollo.

Library of Congress Cataloging-in-Publication Data
Springer, Nancy.
Lionclaw, a tale of Rowan Hood/Nancy Springer.
p. cm.
Sequel to: Rowan Hood, outlaw girl of Sherwood Forest.
Summary: Young Lionel, minstrel in the outlaw band of Rowan Hood, daughter of Robin,
tries to find his courage when she is abducted from Sherwood Forest.
[1. Minstrels—Fiction.   2. Courage—Fiction.   3. Robin Hood (Legendary
character)—Fiction.   4. Adventure and adventurers—Fiction.   5. Middle Ages—Fiction.
6. Great Britain—History—Richard I, 1189–1199—Fiction.]   I. Title.
PZ7.S76846 Ou 2002   [Fic]—dc21   2001045929
ISBN 0-399-23716-X
3 5 7 9 10 8 6 4 2

To Jaime

One

Trudging through Sherwood Forest, with his harp nestled like a turtledove in one big hand, Lionel did not even try to be quiet. It was no use. His feet, the size of pony heads in their curly-tipped shoes, would never learn not to scrape and shuffle. His great lumbering body would never learn not to rustle brush and bracken. And his poor muddled head, seven feet above the ground, would never learn not to conk itself on tree limbs. He made a poor excuse for an outlaw, forsooth.

According to his father, he made a poor excuse for a son altogether.

Lionel slowed, gazing up at tall oaks with acorns fattening on their branches, their autumn leaves hanging muted purple, like old royal velvet, in the twilight. Somewhere high in the darkening sky wild geese bayed like hounds, but Lionel barely heard. Instead, he heard in memory his father's voice: "You disgrace my name. My heir, a sissy, a harp plucker? You are no son of mine. Go. If I see you again, I will kill you."

The words echoed in Lionel's mind. Yes, kill. His father had really said that.

And meant it. Lionel remembered his father's eyes narrowed to slits above his beard, remembered the lion growl in his father's voice. A great lord can, and will, kill whomever he pleases.

My father.

Two years ago he had threatened Lionel with death. *On my birthday.* Thirteenth. Unlucky number.

Lionel sighed, lowered his gaze from the storm-purple oaks, and trudged on. In the months since another powerful man, the Sheriff of Nottingham, had put a bounty on his head, he had become accustomed to the threat of death. But remembering his father saying *You are no son of mine.* He had not yet become accustomed to the heartache.

Or the fear. He often quivered with nerves—oversized, sniveling ninny that he knew himself to be—but he had seldom felt such bone-deep terror as now.

But . . . I have to try.

He slogged on, under the oaks, along a ridge, then into thickets of hemlock and holly, their shadows deepening as night fell. Then down into a rocky dell, where ferns brushed his legs, their fronds dry and yellow at this time of year. Lacework leaves as yellow as primroses, as yellow as Lionel's jerkin; yellow was his favorite color. The butter-bright ferns seemed to glow in the twilight. Gazing at them, Lionel stubbed his toe, stumbled into a boulder, and almost dropped his harp. A blackthorn branch raked his shoulder. His hand, flung out to grab something solid, found only a patch of nettles. "Owww!" he complained.

"Lady have mercy, harper," said a quiet voice in the nightfall. "A deaf man could hear you coming."

Peering into the shadows, Lionel could just make out the gleam of a polished longbow, then behind it the form of a man in green. Uphill from Lionel, motionless and almost invisible amid wild quince and ivy, one of Robin Hood's men was standing guard duty.

Lionel cringed. "Don't shoot me!" he squeaked.

In the dusk he could not see the outlaw's good-humored contempt, but he depended on it, knowing it was there. "Maybe not this time," the man said. "Are you on your way to join the feast?"

Standing still, with the ferns no longer rustling around his shins, Lionel could hear the talk and laughter of the outlaws in their hideout on the other side of the rise.

Seeming to take his silence for ignorance, the guard

3

said, "Robin has brought in a rich lord today, and a dozen of his retainers." To show those whom he robbed that he was no common cutthroat, Robin Hood spared their lives but required them to spend a night with him and his band. "We are giving them our best Sherwood Forest hospitality." Illegal venison, in other words, sauced with humiliation. "But the lord seems not to like it."

Lionel nodded and whispered, "Lord Roderick Lionclaw."

"Aye! Who told you?"

"Will Scathelock." All the outlaws were Lionel's friends, amused by his vast size and timid disposition. "He said Lionclaw fought hard."

"Harder than most, but no match for Robin Hood and his merry men."

Small wonder. Anyone who wanted to join Robin's band had to take on Robin in single combat. One of the many ironies of Lionel's life, he considered, was that he had become an outlaw by helping to save Robin Hood's life, yet he knew himself unworthy to join Robin's band.

No matter. He gave all his fealty to Rowan: Rowan Hood, daughter of Robin Hood. Without looking, Lionel could feel his strand of the band, the silver gimmal ring, hanging inside his jerkin, over his heart.

"I'm here on an errand," he told the guard.

His own errand. Still, he badly wanted not to disgrace Rowan. Or the others.

The guard nodded. Lionel blundered on.

It was almost dark now. It seemed to Lionel that he tripped over every root and stick and stone in Sherwood Forest getting to the top of the rise. But at last he reached a vantage, a crag, where he could see.

There. Robin's hollow.

Under the spreading branches of a giant oak, firelight glinted on two score grinning outlaws decked with the loot from the lord's coffers: fine swords, rich velvets, gold chains. Hoisting flagons of ale, Robin's men sat one-handedly tossing sacks of gold around the circle, roaring with laughter when they dropped the booty. Their captives, the lord's men-at-arms, sat among them, huddled like scared rabbits. Lionel could guess their thoughts: They had been defeated in battle. Their hands had been tied; they had been blindfolded and made to ride backward on their own horses, brought to this place against their will. They were not being hurt now, except for their pride, but once Robin released them, would their lord have them flogged? He had been bound and blindfolded and made to ride backward too. They did not dare to look at him.

From the safety of the trees, Lionel looked.

There. Seated in the place of mocking honor, a throne of piled deerskins near the fire, Lord Roderick Lionclaw.

Father . . .

Lionel felt his heart pounding. Had anything changed in two years? Outwardly, no. Tawny in the firelight, his father's stony face glared out over his jutting beard—the same. His broad-shouldered body, almost as tall as Lionel's, looked as powerful as ever. His hands, battered in many combats, curled as hard as claws, just the way Lionel remembered them. On his men's tabards and his own tunic gleamed Lord Roderick's device, the rampaging golden lion wielding the clawed mace that had made him famous. All the same.

Then Lionel's gaze shifted as a tall outlaw stood up, his curly cap of golden hair glinting in the firelight, his handsome, weather-tanned face alight with firelight and fun. He wore no looted gold, only his customary Lincoln green, his jaunty cap with a tuft of feathers. "Merry men, a toast!" he cried.

The others quieted, looking up to their leader, Robin Hood.

With solemn drollery Robin turned toward Lord Roderick Lionclaw, raising his flagon. "To the continued very excellent health of our honored guest."

"Hear! Hear!" the outlaws cried as Lionclaw gave Robin a glare like a blaze of dragon flame.

Robin seemed not to notice Lionclaw's fiery stare at all. "My good lord," he said in tender tones, "you have not touched your dinner. Are you not feeling well?"

Lionclaw told him, "Go to hell."

The outlaws hooted. Looking on, Lionel felt his gut tighten into a Gordian knot of mixed emotions. He knew what it was to suffer taunts. Yet as often as not, it had been his father who had taunted him.

Robin's mouth pulled down in clownish distress. "My lord is not merry? But consider, my lord, the good you have done this day! Starving peasants will be fed with the gold you have so willingly given—"

"Go fry in hell!"

Lord Lionclaw's yell echoed in the oaks and in Lionel's worst memories, making him shiver. He wanted to crawl away and hide.

I'm a fool to be here.

But—maybe not. Two years ago, when his father had cast him out, he had not known what his singing could do. He had not known that there was enchantment in his voice that could hold a guild hall full of armed men in his power, making them forget their weapons. He had not known that he could sing the badgers out of their dens, silence the nightingales, coax wolf and deer to stand side by side. He had not known that the beauty of his voice could even call forth the *aelfe,* the immortal denizens of the forest, from their hollow hills to listen to him.

Maybe, just maybe, if he sang for his father . . . something might change.

Please, dear Lady, let him . . . let him hear me. . . .

His father's roar echoed away. Robin stood grinning but silent. All the men in the hollow, intent on Robin and Lionclaw, sat silent, awaiting whatever might happen next.

NOW. There would never be a better chance. *Do it!*

Shaking, Lionel set his back against an oak for support. He breathed in. Gently he touched his harp, and the first golden ringing notes quieted his trembling, made him forget the sting of nettles and mockery and hunger, made him forget his father's fury. He cradled his harp, looked out of darkness straight into his father's fiery face, stroked a strong chord out of the harp, lifted his voice, and sang:

> *"In a hollow hill of wild Sherwood*
> *There lives a maiden fair and free,*
> *An archer with a healer's hand*
> *A shining strand in an outlaw band. . . ."*

Praise be to the Lady, his voice flew true, like a golden falcon, like the fragrance of wild roses, like a messenger angel in the night. And his harp strings rang true and honey sweet.

> *". . . This maiden outlaw bold and good*
> *With a wolf who gives her fealty,*
> *Daughter of fitting fatherhood:*
> *Rowan Hood of the rowan wood."*

In the firelit clearing around the great oak tree, outlaws stood or sat motionless, their flagons forgotten in their hands, their faces rapt and turned toward Lionel. Their mouths sagged open, softly agape. But Lionel saw no such softening in his father's face.

Go down there. Let him see you. Face him.

But he could not. Not yet. The thought set him to trembling again. He had to close his eyes against the sight of his father's stony face in order to sing on.

Singing to the dark, he finished the ballad of Rowan Hood and started another, the old, old song that had been his mother's favorite:

> *"Alas, my love, you do me wrong*
> *To cast me off discourteously . . ."*

A lion's roar of rage shattered his song, shook him worse than an earthquake, shook the branches above him. His hands faltered to a halt on his harp, and his throat tightened so badly that he could not sing, only squeak like a mouse. He knew that wordless bellow, although he had hoped never to hear it again.

"How dare you, sirrah!" Words, now, distorted by his father's fury.

With the shards of his song dying around him, Lionel looked. At his father. Lord Roderick Lionclaw, his face blood red in the firelight and creased in an agony of wrath. Lord Roderick Lionclaw, on his feet and lunging toward the darkness. "Churl!" Lionel's father roared, choking with rage. "Shameless! No son of mine! I will kill you!"

Half a dozen of Robin's men leapt to grasp Lord Roderick by the arms. Ablaze with fury, he threw two of them off and surged forward as if the other four were no more than fleas clinging to his hide. Outlaws cried out and seized their quarterstaffs. Linnets and thrushes cried out and flew up from their nests. It seemed to Lionel that the very oaks trembled. He shook so hard, he had to clutch his harp to keep from dropping it.

Three outlaws with quarterstaffs at the ready stood before Lord Roderick, warning him back, but he glared past them at the night, seeming not to see the cudgels. "Disgrace to my name!" he bellowed. "Show yourself!"

Face him, stand up to him! Be a man for once.

"Dare to show yourself, sirrah!" Throwing off the outlaws who held his massive warrior arm, Lionel's father shook his fist as if swinging his clawed mace. "I—will—*kill—you!*"

Lionel heard no more. Without knowing how his feet carried him, how he stood to run, or where he was going, he fled.

His throat had closed. He felt as if he would never be able to sing again.

Two

Lionel awoke with a groan, not understanding at first why his heart ached. He lay wrapped in somebody's woolen mantle, by a fire, and although morning dew sparkled all around him, he felt only warmth. His head pillowed on folded cloth, he gazed up through a grove of wild cherries, their scent sweetening the air, at a dawn sky all the colors of—of birdsong, Lionel thought hazily, for the morning medley of wagtails and thrushes and robins filled the forest. Wild, beautiful music . . . Music. He had tried to give music to— He groaned again, this time remembering why, feeling an even sharper pang as he thought of his father.

"I think I hear something dying," said a familiar, teasing voice.

Lionel sat up to look into Robin Hood's blue, crinkling eyes.

He rubbed his own eyes. "What are you doing here?"

"Here?" Robin quipped, sitting at his ease by the fire, eating cherries, his cap of golden hair haloed by early sunlight. "Where is 'here,' do you know?"

Lionel had no idea where he was, except that it had to be somewhere in the vastness of Sherwood Forest. But there was no need to answer, for around the fire came a slim girl in a kirtle of Lincoln green: Rowan. As silent on her bare feet as a spirit of the forest, she walked to Lionel and knelt by his side, studying him, her dark hair pulled back in a thong of doeskin, her strong, grave face intent on him. Lifting a healing hand, she touched his forehead. How there could be so much teasing in Robin and so much caring in Rowan was one of life's mysteries.

"Are you hungry?" asked another voice. Lionel blinked his bleary eyes and managed to focus on Ettarde, very much the princess even while balancing breakfast on sticks over the fire. With the food under control, she turned her perfect, serene face to Lionel. "Hot bread and cheese," she told him. "Have some?"

He shook his head.

"What! You're not hungry?"

In no mood to be teased about his usually prodigious appetite, Lionel did not respond.

"I'll feed your portion to Tykell," Etty threatened.

Hearing his name, the wolf-dog lifted his head, waving his plumy tail.

"Go ahead," Lionel said.

"Cherries?" Robin asked, offering a handful. "You've led us to a feast of cherries, lad."

Lionel groaned again, mortified, wishing he had not led them to any such place, blundering through the night with no idea they were following. "I suppose I cried myself to sleep?"

"You're entitled," Rowan told him.

"Yes. Cry all you like," Etty said, matter-of-fact. "Are you sure you don't want something to eat?"

"No. Thank you."

"I cannot believe my ears! Is the world ending?"

Ignoring this, Lionel turned to Rowan, meeting her dark eyes. "You heard what happened?"

"We heard and we saw," she said quietly.

"You saw!"

She gifted him with one of her rare smiles. "The sweetest music drew us there, and what did we find? Your father, Lord Lionclaw, forsooth!"

"It is nice to know," Etty said, "that I am not the only so-called aristocrat on the loose in this forest."

Still only half awake, Lionel peered round-eyed at her. "My lady?" Ettarde really *was* a lady—more, a princess, daughter of a petty king. But she had no wish to be reminded of her father, who had tried to force her into marrying.

"Young my lord?" she shot back at Lionel.

"But . . ." Lionel faltered and fell silent, not knowing how to protest. Etty seemed utterly a princess to him, despite the twigs in her hair, but he had never felt himself to be at all a lord.

Rowan saved him from answering. Settling herself cross-legged on the ground, facing him, she ordered, "Tell us."

"Tell you what?"

"How such a brute came to beget you."

Lionel blinked. "Dear me. Usually folk ask how the great Lord Lionclaw came to be afflicted with such a namby-pamby son."

Even to his own ear his tone sounded whining, rife with self-pity—but what matter? He *was* a whiner.

Rowan frowned. Etty gave him one of her expressively placid looks. From his place near the fire Robin said, "Don't ill speak yourself, lad. Just tell us the tale."

"There's little enough to tell." Although it was hard to think where to start. "My father didn't always hate me, I suppose," Lionel said slowly. "He was proud when I was ten years old and already as tall as he." Because his height and strength would make him a great warrior, what else? Every lord's son was destined to spend half his life in battle, and Lord Roderick Lionclaw wanted his firstborn, his Lionel, to be legendary among fighters. "He himself tried to teach me the manly arts of war." Lionel grimaced, remembering those lessons. "Horsemanship was not too terrible . . . although I am too big—I topple over. Kaplunk."

"Kaplunk," Rowan echoed with a wisp of a smile, probably remembering her own horseback ride to save Robin.

"Falling off a horse is only moderately bad," Lionel said. "But the lance, the sword . . ." He felt his mouth softening, his lips trembling. "He came at me with that great monstrous clawed mace, and I *screamed*. I *ran away*. I thought I did well not to soil myself, but he thought not. He *beat me*."

Lionel looked at Robin Hood, expecting to see pity and contempt in his eyes, but Robin was looking past him. Lionel turned to see the wild boy walking into camp carrying several large trout. Skinny, half-naked, shaggy-haired oddling that he was, the wild boy caught fish with his bare hands and seemed to think nothing of it. Silent as usual, he nodded at Lionel, knelt by the fire, drew his knife, and started gutting the fish.

Lionel looked away. Guts, even fish guts, turned his

stomach. It was as his father said: He was a shame, a disgrace.

Etty said, "I think I'd run too if Lord Roderick Lionclaw were coming at me with his mace."

Lionel gave her his best simpering stare. "But you're not seven feet tall, my dear lady."

"I'm not your dear—"

Another voice intervened. "Did our great Lord Roderick try to beat the music out of you?" asked Robin Hood.

Lionel glanced at him in surprise; he had not expected such understanding of Robin. What had been Robin's experience of a father? It was hard to imagine he had ever had one.

Rowan, sitting so quietly—her father was Robin Hood himself, but she had not known him for the first thirteen years of her life, and he had not known he had a daughter.

Ettarde—her father had educated her like a scholar, then tried to marry her off to the highest bidder. Fathers—half of anyone's life seemed to be about who had fathered them.

I'm not the only one with father problems.

Yes, his father had tried to beat the music out of him. Many times. But Lionel put on a bland face.

"Music? My dear fellow, why would he want to beat me for that?"

Robin grinned. "Why indeed?"

"Who taught you to play the harp and sing, Lionel?" Rowan asked.

"My mother." His heart leapt like a wounded deer at the thought of her, his tall, gentle mother always stooping to make herself seem smaller. "She was from the Western Isles. Magical lands, folk say. This was her harp." Lionel touched the instrument nestled in its own blanket by his side, its mellow waxed wood carved like a wreath of ivy leaves. His heart swelled as he remembered how her back straightened when she took up her harp, how her timid blue eyes widened and gazed fearlessly, how the music had widened her shoulders and swelled the pillar of her throat. "When she sang and played, the finches gathered at the window to listen."

"And your father?" asked Rowan quietly. "Did he listen?"

"No."

In the silence that followed, he heard crisp leaves rustling, starlings quarreling over cherries, squirrels chattering about acorns. Deeper in the forest a wolf whined. Tykell raised his head and yawned. Etty tossed him the remaining bread and cheese. The wild boy scraped the last of the scales off the gutted fish, wrapped them in dock leaves, laid the packets on the embers of the fire, and sat nearby, warming himself.

Robin Hood said to Lionel, "There will always be a few like that, won't there? Guy of Gisborn." They all had black memories of Gisborn, outlaw hunter who could not be ensorcelled by Lionel's music. "And now Lord Roderick Lionclaw."

"Yes."

"Where is your mother now, lad?"

"Dead. She died of fever when I was twelve."

A murmur of sorrow went around the circle by the cooking fire. Lionel saw Rowan's face shadow as she remembered, perhaps, her own mother's death. And Etty—her mother was alive, although likely Etty would never see her again. The wild boy—did he have a mother?

But it didn't matter. Mothers had no power.

"And when I was thirteen," Lionel added, "my father told me to go my ways or he would kill me. So I went away. He did not want a harp plucker for his son and heir, and who can blame him?"

"I blame him," said Rowan.

Ettarde asked, "Lionel—was it the music that turned your father against you, or the music that made you defy him?"

Lionel felt his heart shrink. He peered at her just like his mother at her most nearsighted. "My *dear* little lady," he protested.

"I may be little, but I'm not your dear lady!"

"But dear goodness me, which came first, the chicken or the egg?"

"Lionel." It was Rowan, her level gaze on him demanding truth. "It's a good question. Answer it."

He groaned, closed his eyes in protest, and tried to think. Remembering: Father, the horseback riding lessons, swordplay and spear play and that great awful mace. And then his thirteenth birthday, and Father expecting as a matter of course that he, young Lord Lionel, would be a man and a lord's son, put on the Lionclaw tabard, and let himself be drubbed by the men-at-arms and . . . and if he weren't such a great blubbering sissy, it might have happened too, he might be a fighter now, a knight, instead of an outlaw minstrel. But had he always been such a coward, or was it the music that had made him be, or . . .

It was too hard to remember how it had all happened. He opened his eyes and faced Rowan's steady look studying him. He said, "I was so big, every man jack in the castle was always and forever wanting me to fight. But—" He felt tears welling up in his eyes and a babyish whine in his voice. "But I didn't *want to*."

Rowan said nothing. Her thoughtful gaze on him neither called him a coward nor excused him.

Her wolf-dog, Tykell, raised his head, his velvety ears pricked, stared southward, and growled deep in his massive chest. In the same breath every thrush and starling in the cherry trees cried out and flew up in a flurry of wings. Squirrels chittered, and in the tops of the oaks, rooks crowed an alarm. Then silence cut through Sherwood like a scream, and in the silence Lionel heard a steel-shod hoof clang against stone.

Three

As quickly as the starlings had flown, all those by the fire leapt up, reached for their weapons, then ran and vanished amid the trees. Struggling to his feet, Lionel blundered after them, panic galloping in his chest. Where could he go? Rowan and Robin and the others had a knack for disappearing like spirits in the woods, moving silently, their slim bodies in brown leggings and green jerkins almost invisible, at one with oak and blackthorn. *But I stick out!* Too big, too bright in his foppish yellow tunic and red hose, Lionel crashed like a charging boar through bracken and fallen cherry leaves, and even through the roaring in his ears he could hear hoofbeats near, nearer—

Someone grabbed his hand—Rowan. "This way." She towed him at a run into the oaks, then whispered, "Down!" and shoved him flat on the ground. She threw her brown mantle over him and strewed him with leaves. Lionel heard Tykell close by, growling like a hive of bees. Rowan slipped behind an oak near Lionel's head, bow and arrow at the ready, motionless. From where he lay on his belly in damp loam, with his face in mushrooms and last year's rotting leaves, Lionel could see all too near at hand the campfire from which he had just fled—

He just barely kept himself from screaming as a black monster horse with two heads leapt over the fire.

Or so it seemed at first—a monster, a two-headed black horse thing, an apparition worthy of a very bad night's sleep. It was Guy of Gisborn, the kingdom's most infamous bounty hunter, on his giant black steed in his armor of black horsehide, his thin-lipped face visored by the dead horse's head, mane and ears and sunken eyes and all.

Broadsword in hand, Gisborn slashed at the campfire as if it had offended him, scattering the blazing sticks. With his other hand he curbed his lathered steed, his black-gloved fist hauling the reins. "Sirrah minstrel!" he roared to the forest, his voice booming out from under the black horse skull that shadowed his face. "Coward harp plucker!"

From a dense stand of oak and elm beyond Gisborn floated three clear, silver notes—Robin Hood's horn summoning his merry men to his aid. And also, Lionel realized with a swelling of his heart, letting Gisborn know that "sirrah minstrel" had help and friends.

With a snarl Gisborn wheeled his foaming steed. "So, the cock-robin bow plucker too?" he shouted. "Bah. My curse on you and all your so-called merry men." Gisborn's prancing, frightened horse circled the fire as Gisborn glared into the forest all around him. "Sirrah so-called minstrel! Come forth and face me before I slay you and all your outlaw friends."

Face Guy of Gisborn? Not likely, not anytime soon, thankee very much. Trembling, pressing his face deeper into the leaves, Lionel felt Gisborn's glance rake the oaks and fix on him—no, it swept past. He felt a whimper rising in his throat and gritted his teeth to keep it down. He felt as if he might be sick.

"*Lion*-el." Gisborn's snarling voice made a mockery of the name. "I know you're there. I can smell your fat, craven, quaking body. Show yourself!"

Craven and quaking sounded accurate, although fat did not—but why argue over trifles? Jaw clenched, Lionel lay still through a listening silence. Only echoes and the rustling of dry leaves in the breeze answered Gisborn.

"Well," said the outlaw hunter in a softer, even nastier voice, "I think your mother was no honest woman, harp plucker."

Odd how a spasm of rage could blot out fear and good sense. Under the mantle that blanketed him, Lionel's fists clenched. A voice no louder than the breeze in the leaves whispered, "Lie still." Rowan.

"Therefore I title thee bastard, harp plucker," Gisborn's voice boomed, "for surely you are not your father's son. And when I find you and take you prisoner, I shall bloody your back with the flat of my sword, for you are a low-born churl, not worthy of my blade. You and any other vermin outlaw lurking in my hearing. Farewell for now, bastards all." Gisborn spurred his horse into a low rear, wheeled, and leapt over the remnants of the fire. The horse screamed as it galloped away.

Lionel let out his breath with a gasp almost like a sob.

"Stay where you are," Rowan whispered.

He obeyed her. But as if Guy of Gisborn and all his threats meant nothing, the wild boy walked out of hiding and crouched by the fire, searching the ashes with his bare hands.

Rowan watched, then relaxed, lowering her bow. Aloud, she said, "Toads have mercy." It was her favored oath, and Lionel often wondered where she had gotten it. Toads, for goodness' sake? But Rowan seldom swore by anything stronger. "Toads," she complained again of the wild boy, "he wants his breakfast. Get up, Lionel. Your hair is full of leaves."

"Your father sent him," said the wild boy, his low voice as burry as a thistle.

Safe in an oak grove on their way back to the rowan hollow where they lived, Lionel and Rowan and Ettarde had been talking of Gisborn when the wild boy forsook the fish he was gnawing and spoke. Lionel stared at him. Rowan and Etty stared. Even Tykell raised his furry head and stared. Through black hair that fell over his eyes, as shaggy as a moorland pony's forelock, the wild boy stared back, a cooked, cold, somewhat trampled trout in his hands.

"I heard," he said in answer to their stares.

They waited for more. The wild boy gulped fish.

"Heard what?" Rowan prompted after a while. "Where?"

"Fountain Dale."

"You were fishing in the stream below Fountain Dale?"

The wild boy spit out trout bones and tossed them over his shoulder before nodding. He had no manners and almost no clothing. Bare legs, bare feet with soles almost as hard as horn. Lionel wondered whether the wild boy would go barefoot all winter.

"And?" Rowan urged.

"Gisborn stopped to water his horse."

"Toads! Did he see you?"

The wild boy answered only with a look: Of course not. He threw aside the mangled spine of one trout and reached for another. He said, "On the Nottingham Way came Lionclaw in a rage, his men shaking."

No wonder. Knowing his father, Lionel could picture it: Lord Roderick in a cold fury, he and his retainers sent on their way with much merry mockery by Robin Hood's men. And once the outlaws were gone, Lord Roderick lashing out at his men-at-arms with words and likely with the flat of his sword as well.

"I listened," said the wild boy, and he turned to Lionel. He had strange eyes, dark and hot, like the coals of a fire. He gazed but did not speak.

Lionel felt his heart hammering, and he did not like it, this woods colt keeping him on tenterhooks. With his best pout he simpered, "Well, tell me what they said, my dear fellow."

"Don't call me that."

"Then say your name!" Lionel's anger leapt out of him, a surprise to him as much as anyone. He leaned toward the wild boy. "You are a member of the band." On the wild boy's skinny, naked chest, suspended on a thong of deerhide, gleamed the silver circle that said so. "You know our names; tell us yours!"

Silence. Lionel heard acorns falling, crows calling, a chill autumn wind hissing through the oaks. He wished he had not said so much or shown so much. His sudden anger had changed his voice, making it deeper, surer, more like his father's; this was not good. He felt the others give him curious looks, and something made him pull his big bony knees to his chest, curling himself up like a huge hedgehog.

Still staring at him with eyes like black embers, the wild boy said a single word: "Rook."

"Rook?"

"Yes."

"That's your name?"

"Yes."

Lionel had his whine back now. "But a rook's a bird, my—" He stopped himself from saying "dear fellow."

"Yes," said the wild boy, "and a lion is a beast."

Rowan's quiet voice said, "Rook. That's a guardian bird. It's a good name."

"The rook is a cousin of the crow and the jackdaw," said Etty with a quirk in her voice, mocking her own scholarly knowledge. She put aside her portion of fish, placing it tidily upon a dock leaf, and wiped her hands on a muslin kerchief she kept tucked in her sleeve for that purpose. Meanwhile, she held forth with a smile. "The word 'rook' also signifies a watchtower and the chess piece more commonly known as a castle."

Rowan turned to Etty, bright-eyed. "Lion," she urged. "What do you know about lions? Are they real?"

"Of course not," Lionel complained before Ettarde could answer. "Who has ever seen a lion? They're like unicorns. I'd rather be named after anything else."

As if he had not spoken, Etty reported to Rowan, "According to Pliny the Elder in his *Natural History,* the lion sleeps with his eyes open, roams barren wilderness, fears nothing but scorpions, and charms his prey by drawing a circle in the sand with his barbed tail."

Rowan exclaimed, "He has those great teeth and great claws, yet he *charms* his prey?"

"Somebody tell that to my father," Lionel grumbled. "There's nothing charming about him." His heart panged as if it would never stop hurting when he spoke of his father.

And it was too much to expect, now that he had shouted at him, that the wild boy—Rook—the woods brat squatting there mumbling fish grease all over himself—too much to expect that he would now vouchsafe his news. But no harm trying.

Lionel said to him, "Rook." Proffering the name like a peace offering. "You said my father sent Gisborn to frighten me."

Rowan picked up a stick of kindling wood and pulled her hunting knife from its deerhide sheath at her belt. Watching her start to whittle, Lionel knew she was thinking hard, if not quite worried.

Without missing a bite, the wild boy looked up at Lionel, the whites of his eyes flashing under his dark brows. "No."

"No? But you said—"

"No, not frighten you. Kill you."

Four

I can't," Lionel said, shivering from standing in cold drizzle. He detested wet autumn weather. He loathed the sodden leaves falling from the trees and clinging to his feet; he hated the bare drippy rattling branches overhead, and the dank wind that made them rattle, and the gray sky. He wanted to settle beside a warm hearth with a flagon of mulled cider in his hand, but what he actually had was a smoky cave to go home to. He hated being outlawed, with the Sheriff of Nottingham's insulting price, one hundred pounds, on his head. He hated Sherwood Forest. He hated bows and arrows and the stick Rowan had notched as a mark for him to shoot at. He hated almost everything except Rowan.

The drizzle fell on Rowan too, slowly soaking her sable-brown hair and her brown mantle, but she didn't seem to mind any more than if she were a young wolf, or the wolf-dog, Tykell, lying near her feet.

With a borrowed longbow and a sheaf of yard-long arrows in her hands, Rowan stared at Lionel. "Can't? You haven't even tried."

He said, "It's no use. I can't learn to kill people. I'm a coward."

"Coward?" Rowan's stare hardened, but her voice grew more mild. "I seem to remember that not so long ago, you fought an armored knight with your bare hands to save a girl you didn't even know. . . ."

"That was different. He was hitting Etty. It made me mad."

"And then you risked your life and got yourself outlawed for helping me—"

"But my dear Rowan, I didn't *shoot* anyone."

"Your *dear* father would gladly shoot you. Why—"

"It's not my fault!" Lionel felt his voice spiral into a squeal. "I can't help it if my *jackass* father—"

Tykell raised his head and growled.

Stiffening, Rowan breathed at Lionel, "Shhh!" Head up, scanning the woods all around her, listening, even whiffing the wind, she stood hearkening like a deer for any hint of danger. In the few days since Lord Roderick Lionclaw's involuntary stay at Robin's camp, it seemed as if all the bounty hunters in the kingdom had converged on Sherwood Forest like vultures on a carcass. Plague take them all, they were gathering even worse than they were wont to do after one of Robin's escapades caused the Sheriff of Nottingham to increase the reward for that famous outlaw's head.

Tykell scrambled to his feet and stood stiff-legged, his neck hairs bristling. Rowan laid aside the oversized longbow borrowed from Little John and grabbed her own bow from where it leaned with her quarterstaff against a young ash tree, close at hand. In one quick movement she set the tip of her bow against her instep, strung it, and pulled an elf bolt from the sheaf on her back, nocking it to the bowstring.

But then Tykell relaxed and wagged his shaggy tail. A wagtail whistled. At least it sounded like a wagtail to Lionel. But Rowan breathed out and lowered her bow. A moment later Robin's second in command, Little John—all seven feet of him—appeared behind a rift of hornbeam trees, quarterstaff in hand. As he strode nearer, swinging the six-foot oaken cudgel like a walking stick, he scanned Lionel and nodded approval. His rugged face softened with a smile. "We'll make an outlaw of you yet, lad."

Lionel could not answer the smile. He appreciated that the clothing he wore, a shabby brown jerkin and leggings Little John had lent him, kept him from standing out like a popinjay in the woods, but he did not feel like himself in them. And he did not consider that he would ever be an outlaw—not the way Little John meant.

"How goes the archery?" Little John asked, halting beside Rowan but looking at Lionel for his answer.

It was Rowan who answered. "It goes not at all, yet." She spoke as levelly as if she were discussing the weather. "What news, Little John?"

He lost his smile. "The king's foresters are on the hunt for us as never before," he said, lowering his voice as if fate might be listening. "They have set man traps."

Lionel did not understand, but he saw Rowan's weather-tanned face go pale.

"Be careful," Little John said.

Rowan nodded.

Lionel burst out, "What is it?" He had not seen her look so stricken since the day Robin Hood had been captured.

She turned to him blankly for a moment before she told him, "Steel traps, the kind furriers use, but big. Meant for outlaws."

"And not meant kindly either," said Little John. "Much the Miller's Son found one this morning—with his left leg."

"No! Is it—"

"Broken."

Lionel felt a chill worse than the cold drizzle trickling down his back. He felt sickness start to knot in the pit of his stomach.

"It could have been worse," Little John added. "We heard him scream. He did not bleed to death before we found him. Or lie there and starve."

Rowan whispered, "What can we do?"

"Not much, lass. Stay off the trails, even deer trails. Watch for piled leaves—that's how they hide them. And feel your way, like this." Little John lifted his quarterstaff and prodded the ground in front of him.

Wind soughed like a snake in the oaks, shaking the branches. A few laggard acorns fell like stones. The drizzle turned to rain. A cold sickness filled Lionel's chest and rose in his throat like bile. He hated it. He blurted, "Don't blame me! It's not my fault!"

Rowan gave him a frowning look. Little John said, "Why, no one said it was, lad."

"You're thinking it is. The foresters—you all think my father sent them. Because of me."

Her voice weary, Rowan said, "Lionel, don't be an idiot."

But Little John turned on him. "It is true that your father has the king's ear, is it not?"

Lionel stood taut and sickened, not answering.

"It doesn't matter," Rowan said. "There will always be enemies, Lionel."

"True enough," said Little John. "And you must be ready for them, lad. Now show me what you can do with my second-best bow."

The bow Rowan had borrowed from him. Likely the only bow in the forest big enough for Lionel. They wanted him to learn . . . but he couldn't. He just couldn't do it. They'd have him swinging a sword next.

Lionel stepped back and shook his head.

"We'd better go," Rowan said in her quiet way. "No use soaking your second-best bow in the rain."

But bows got wet in the rain commonly enough. That was what they were waxed for, to protect them. Little John gave Rowan a quizzical glance, then asked Lionel, "Can't you hit the mark yet, lad? It's only ten paces away."

Lionel mumbled, "I can't learn weapons."

"What?"

"I can't learn *weapons*!" His voice rose almost to a squeal, setting crows to cawing in the treetops.

"Rubbish." Little John lifted his quarterstaff, twirled it, and feinted at Lionel. "Defend yourself. Rowan, give him your staff, lass."

Lionel exclaimed, "No!"

"Yes." With the tip of the oaken staff, Little John hit his chest a light blow, just a tap really, but it hurt. Rowan grabbed her quarterstaff and thrust it toward Lionel.

"No. I won't touch it." Lionel shoved his hands behind his back.

"What, you'd rather let me drub you?" Little John twirled his staff and struck Lionel on the leg. "Are you afraid of me?"

Silly question. Anybody with the sense of a goat would be afraid of Little John, as tough as his yew bow and the tallest outlaw in Robin Hood's band, almost Lionel's height—just about the same height as Lord Roderick Lionclaw, actually. Lionel did not answer. With his hands behind him, he backed away and thought of running—but the way things were going, he would catch his big feet on a root, trip, and fall headfirst into a man trap. He had to stay, and—why was it all happening again?

Little John thwacked him in the ribs. The blows were getting harder, although not yet as hard as some of the beatings he had suffered as a boy and a lord's son, forsooth. Rowan thrust her quarterstaff toward him again, and Little John urged, "Take it, *Lamb*-el!"

The mockery in his voice made Lionel's eyes start to sting. He shook his head hard and flung himself to the ground, whipping his hands around to tuck them under his belly, curling his knees up to his chest.

"Stand up and fight, coward!" Little John sounded angry now. All too much like an angry father with a stick in his hand. Lionel clenched his teeth as he felt Little John strike him a hard blow on the part of him that was sticking out the most.

"Stop it!" Rowan's voice.

Lionel heard quarterstaff clash against quarterstaff. He looked up. Rowan had stepped between him and Little John with her staff raised between both hands, parrying the tall outlaw's next blow.

Head and shoulders taller than she, probably twice her weight, Little John tried to reach over her to strike Lionel again. She caught the blow on her staff; Lionel saw it rock her, but she did not give way, not even an inch.

Little John blinked, then stepped back and lowered his quarterstaff. "By the Lady," he told Rowan, "you're bold."

Breathing hard, she kept her staff at the ready and did not answer. Lionel could not see her face.

"Too bad you can't give some of your courage to that lunk." Little John jerked his head toward Lionel.

Still on the ground, Lionel felt several different emotions making a broth in him, heating his eyes and face, making his nose run. He sat up and blew it between his fingers onto the wet leaves.

He heard Rowan say, "Lionel has his own kind of courage."

"Bah. Rowan, if you know what's good for your band, you'll send him away."

Rowan lowered her staff, shook her head, and said, "Toads take it. Little John—"

"You're too softhearted, Rowan. Send him away before he's the death of you all." Little John nodded a curt farewell at her, ignoring Lionel, and strode off between the naked, shivering trees, kicking over the stick Rowan had set up for Lionel to shoot at.

Cold to the bone, with rain trickling from his hair down his neck, soaking wet from lying in the loam, Lionel got up. From sky and treetops crows yelled their mocking calls, telling any forester or bounty hunter in the area, *Here he is, the big sissy!* Rowan stood watching Little John walk out of sight beyond the hornbeams. Then she sighed and scanned all around her, checking for danger. Lionel tried to brush loam and leaves off his jerkin, but the wet stuff just smeared and dirtied his hands. His leg hurt, his chest hurt, other parts of him hurt where Little John had struck him, and he did not know what to say to Rowan.

Finally he said, "Thank you."

"Rotten miserable no-neck toads," she grumbled without looking at him. She picked up her bow, Little John's bow, and the borrowed arrows. "Let's go. Just watch where you walk."

Five

Sheltering from the night with the others in the rowan hollow, Lionel lay with his feet cramped against stone because he was too big to fit in there any other way. *All my life,* he thought, bone weary and trying to sleep under a deerskin that only half covered him, *all my life, cursed to be big.* Everyone trying to make a fighter out of him just because he was over-sized. Infamous because he had swung at a knight and missed and knocked down a horse instead. Doomed to be killed by some bounty hunter because he was too big to hide. Hated by his own father—

No. Don't think about it anymore.

In the space allotted to him, he turned himself over with a sigh and became aware of Rowan's voice, low. ". . . here with us?" she was saying. "So far it's been safe here."

"Only because there are so few of you." It sounded like Robin Hood. With his bleary eyes half lidded, Lionel looked. He hadn't thought he had slept, but yes, sometime while he wasn't noticing, Robin Hood had come visiting. From where he lay, Lionel had a sideward view of Rowan and Robin huddled by the small campfire, looking like a pair of weary angels in its muted glow, with the rowan trees rising beyond them. Scarlet berries swung in clusters on the slender rowans and dotted the mossy boulders that formed a wall all around. From a cleft in the rocks the spring flowed as sweet and pure as a maiden's dreams. This was a maiden's secret place, this woodland hollow; it was Rowan's. Granddaughter of the aelfe, she was in a very real way the spirit of this place.

By her side lay Tykell, firelight turning his gray fur golden. Beyond the fire Etty and Rook sat leaning against stone, listening. Lionel did not feel like sitting up. He closed his eyes again.

". . . always have springwater," Rowan was saying, "and we have dried meat and fish stored away. There are a thousand small caves and hiding places in the rocks—"

"Thank you, Rowan, my brave heart, but no," Robin said. "If our enemies have not yet hunted among these crags, it is because they have not yet seen the smoke of a cooking fire. Bring in two score merry men, and that will change. No, I've made up my mind. But I'll ask again, won't you go with us?"

Her voice full of thought, Rowan said, "All the way to Barnesdale Forest?"

"Perhaps. A bird on the wing is harder to bring down. And the farther we fly, the harder for anyone to bag us."

Rowan did not reply. In the night Lionel heard no sounds except the breeze in the rowans and the whispering of the fire. Not even wolf song, not even owl hoot or fox yelp or leaves rustling. Lonesome silence. For a moment Lionel thought of his harp, of warming that silence with ringing notes, of the strings singing under his big fingers, and the thought made his heart pang with longing and grief. His father . . . Lionel had not been able to play his harp since that fateful night. There was a hole in his heart where music should have been, a dry emptiness where once there had been a wellspring of song.

"Ettarde?" Rowan was saying, looking at the others. "Rook? What do you think?"

What about me? Lionel thought, and then he realized Rowan thought he was sleeping. Just as well. If it had not been for his folly, trying to woo his father with music, Robin Hood would not be fleeing now.

Ettarde said slowly, "My mind tells me yes, Robin is right—to stay clear of the hunters it is better to be on the move. But my heart tells me to stay."

On Rowan's firelit face Lionel saw a flicker of a smile that seemed to say Rowan thought and felt much the same as Ettarde. Rowan asked, "So which will you follow, head or heart?"

"I don't know."

"Rook?"

The wild boy just shrugged.

Robin Hood said to Rowan, "You're their leader—"

"No, I'm not. We're each a strand of the band—"

"Nonsense, lass, and this just goes to show it. You are the one who must decide—"

Lionel rolled his eyes. Who did he think he was, badgering her? A pox take him.

Lionel sighed, groaned, sat up, and turned to warm his cramped feet by the fire. Without even a nod at Robin, he said to Rowan, "You want to stay, don't you?"

Yes, just by the way her warm gaze fixed on him, he knew he was right. But she challenged, "What makes you say that?"

"You are Rowan Hood of the rowan wood." Lionel's glance took in the hidden hollow, the spring, the rowans. "This grove is your second self. You'd be uprooted without it."

"And what if she's dead within it?" snapped Robin Hood.

Lionel gave him a blank stare. "Why, my dear fellow—"

"Stop that, Lionel!" Ettarde's voice.

Her command startled him almost silent. "Goodness," he murmured, peering at her.

But she shot a quelling look at him, then said to Robin, "Do you really think we're in more danger here? Or is it just that you're annoyed?"

"Annoyed at me, perhaps?" Lionel inquired, owlish.

"Now why ever would I be annoyed at you, my dear little fellow?" Robin mocked, mimicking Lionel. Without waiting for a reply, he said to Ettarde in his usual quiet tones, "Probably no more danger than usual. It's just that I'd rather have my daughter by me." He turned to Rowan. "But you must follow your heart, lass."

"You know my heart's with you. But what of Much?" The outlaw whose leg had been broken in the man trap, Lionel remembered, shuddering. "Can he travel?"

"We'll make shift to carry him along."

"No. He'll be the worse for it. Bring him here and leave him with us. I'll see to his healing."

Robin looked long at her. "So that's your answer," he said finally. "You'll stay here."

She gazed back at him without replying.

"As you must, lass. Do as you must." Robin smiled at her, but the smile did not seem to reach his eyes; they looked gray and shadowed. He rose and pulled the hood of his mantle over his head, but then he stood just beyond the fire. He took a long breath. "Much would pine if we left him behind," he told Rowan, his by-the-way tone belied by the taut look on his face. "We'll manage. Many thanks for your offer, lass—but if you wish to do me a favor, I'll ask you this: Might I borrow Lionel to travel with us?"

Lionel sat straight up. "What?" he squeaked.

But Robin looked only at Rowan. "I'm likely to have need of a big, strong man," he told her.

She smiled such a wide, warm smile as Lionel had seldom seen on her face, as warm as an embrace. "Father," she told Robin Hood tenderly, "don't try your foxy ways on me. What do you want Lionel for, really?"

Robin blinked but did not reply. Lionel bleated, "He wants to make cudgel meat of me!"

Robin Hood turned on him, whipping his mantle hood back from his fierce face. "You great oaf, are you

45

going to hide behind her forever? You'll bring Lord Roderick's army down on her!"

"*Father,*" Rowan ordered, "hush." She stood to face him more levelly, still gifting him with her rare smile. "Have some faith in the forest," she told him.

"Bosh." But he lowered his eyes.

"You know it's not bosh. You know the aelfe will have a care for me. And you know I wouldn't send Lionel away even if he were mine to send. May the Lady watch over you."

She lifted both hands in a sort of blessing, and his stance softened. He lowered his head, and she touched his blond hair. He kissed her lightly on the forehead, then without a word or even the sound of a rustling leaf he turned and strode away, lost from sight within a moment in the night.

Six

S top it, Lionel!" Ettarde hissed between clenched
teeth. "Idiot, they're nowhere near us."

Her ire, unusual for her, actually made him cease
whimpering. Crouched close beside her in the dank
hollow left by a fallen plane tree, hiding under its up-
turned roots, he peered at her. Her hair, chopped off
when she had disguised herself as a boy, now straggled
to her shoulders, too long for comfort and too short to
tie back; his own fawn-colored curls hung longer. Dirt
streaked her hands, her face, her frock, from the wake-
robin root she and Lionel had been gathering. Perhaps
she was not feeling like a princess today. Why should
she? Eating roots, hunted like a rabbit . . .

No, she was being hunted like a rare prize, a uni-
corn, to be captured. And he was being hunted like a
wolf, for the price on his head. Bounty hunters. Lionel

felt himself start to whimper again. "But my dear Etty," he whispered, "they could be *anywhere*!"

"We know where they are. We heard them coming. We saw them go by."

Yes, and Lionel shuddered to think of them: three grim, bearded men on shaggy horses, their weapons clanking, one of them with a freshly severed human head fastened by the hair to his saddle. If Robin had hoped to draw the bounty hunters away from Rowan, it hadn't worked. In the week since he and his men had started northward, each day had seemed more fearsome than the one before.

"The crows have stopped yelling," Etty muttered, still sounding cross. Perhaps it was the idea of eating wake-robin root that was vexing her. The stuff was awful, but with sheriff's men and king's men and bounty hunters swarming the forest, trying to hunt deer was too dangerous.

"Stay here till dark," Lionel said.

"No. Come on." With one hand gathering her apron full of the wretched roots and the other in the dirty dead leaves, Etty started to get up.

"No!" Lionel whispered, grabbing her arm to keep her down. "No, I'm scared!"

"Stop that." Flinging off his hand, Etty flounced to a seat on the mossy edge of the hollow, glaring at him.

"Lionel, I'm tired of that whining sissy act of yours. Stop it right now."

He could not have felt more astonished if she had turned into a fox and bitten him. He gawked at her. "Act? But my dear—"

She snatched a root from her apron as if to fling it at him. "I'm not your dear anything! And you *are* a big sham."

Something deep within him went very quiet, taut, and still, like a wolf tensed to leap. The sudden watchful silence in his heart bewildered him as much as her words.

Staring at her, he murmured, "I don't understand."

She gazed back at him, sighed, and lowered her hand slowly, laying down the root as if she were relinquishing a weapon. With her usual ladylike calm she said, "Think back to when you were a boy. They wanted to make you be a fighter. But you loved your music above all things, and they would have taken that away from you. So you came up with a plan—"

"No. Stop it."

She did not stop. "You acted like a mincing sissy so they would give up on you. I can see it. Red tights and a yellow tunic, forsooth, and you grew your hair long, and then you got yourself a crisping tong to make sure it curled—"

49

He had forgotten about the crisping tong, but now he remembered, and it was as if she had second sight. It shook him. He exclaimed, "But I *am* a coward! A lord's son is supposed to love swordplay and all the rest of it, but I— Fighting terrifies me."

"Why?"

"Because I'll hurt my hands!"

Then Lionel gasped, wishing he could snatch back the words, wishing he could swallow them. But it was too late. Truth had leapt out of him. He gulped, hearing a distant hawk scream, hearing a chill wind rustling the last few leaves on the oaks, seeming to hear Ettarde and all of Sherwood Forest listening to his words flying like golden arrows into the white wintry sky.

With her clear eyes upon him, once more the poised princess, Ettarde nodded and said, "See? You have a perfectly good reason. Why call yourself a coward?"

"But I *am*—"

"It's not cowardice to protect your hands. They could have been maimed. Fingers lopped off."

In his mind's eye Lionel saw his father's hard hands, broken and bloodied in combat until they had stiffened into lion claws fit only to grip shield and sword. Or mace. That great, fearsome mace.

"And then you wouldn't be able to play your harp anymore," Etty continued. "Isn't that it, Lionel?"

"Yes," he admitted. With an ache in his heart he wondered, would he ever play his harp again? There was no music in him these days.

"So you defied your father to keep your music," Etty said quietly. "Nothing could be braver. How can you call yourself a coward?"

"But . . . I am. . . ." A big sham? It was true what Etty said about the hair and the clothes. He remembered now how he had done it so they would stop trying to make him fight. And it was true that his sissiness had started as an act; a few times he had actually faked a faint when someone came at him with a sword. And yes, it was true that he had defied his father in a way, and he had been on his own, cast out, even before that fat, stupid sheriff had outlawed him—but if all this was true, why did he feel like such a mouse? What about the way he whined, and simpered, and whimpered, as naturally as he breathed? If he hadn't always been a sissy, surely he had become one by now.

The sky had darkened; the wind was rising. Through the bare crowns of the oaks Lionel could see wolfish clouds scudding beneath the white belly of the sky. And he still felt his trembling terror of the bounty hunters, no matter what Ettarde said.

"You are Lionel of the Rowan Band," Ettarde told him, "and I'll thank you to remember it."

Then she froze, looking around her and listening. Sticks scraped and rattled as something moved in the forest, and not too far away a black flurry of crows flew up, barking. Deer made the brush rattle, but crows did not take alarm at deer. "They're coming back this way," she whispered.

Lionel cowered, his heart hammering. "Get *down!*"

"No. They might look harder this time." Ettarde grabbed his arm and yanked it. "Come on!" Running, she led off toward the safety of the rocks.

But as they reached the edge of the craggy uplands that surrounded the rowan hollow, a roar jolted them to a halt. Man roar, beast roar—it was hard to separate the man's fierce shout, all too much like Lord Lion-claw's, from a wolfish snarl.

And then came a cry, almost a scream: "No! Stop where you are!" Rowan's voice.

Dropping a heap of wake-robin roots, Etty darted toward the sound of Rowan in trouble. Clenching his teeth to hold back his fluttering heart from flying right out of his mouth, Lionel loped after her, following her lead as she hid behind a cascade of ivy to look.

There stood a squat toad of a red-haired man wearing the tabard and helm of a forester. Viewing the back of his neck, Lionel saw red bristles like those of a wild boar. Charming fellow. With his short, heavy brute of a hacking sword drawn, he had Rowan and Tykell cornered against a wall of rock. Rowan held him off with drawn bow, but from the swaggering way he held himself, he seemed to know that she, the healer, was reluctant to harm; she could have shot him before now. Or perhaps he had small regard for a half-grown lass. The wolf-dog snarling by her side probably gave him more pause.

"Step back," Rowan told him, "or I *will* plant an arrow in you. Right there." Her narrowed eyes indicated the soft spot just above his navel.

But the forester laughed like a cuckoo. " 'Step back,' forsooth," he mimicked. "Step back from a suckling dairymaid? I think not. But you're small game, girl." His voice dropped mockery, became covetous. "It's big game I want. The overgrown popinjay, Lionclaw's son. Tell me where he is, and I'll let you go."

"No," Rowan blurted. Then Lionel saw her face wince as she realized she had betrayed herself.

" 'No,' forsooth? Come, lass." Lionel could hear triumph in the man's tone. Then his voice lowered, conspiratorial. "You know where he is, don't you? Lead me to him, and I'll share Lionclaw's bounty with you. A thousand pounds, gold!"

A thousand pounds? The enormity of his father's hatred made Lionel's mind reel like a mob of crows.

No wonder every bounty hunter in the kingdom was after him.

The forest had gone charcoal dark, storm clouds bellying low enough to shroud the crags, the treetops. Wind hissed like a giant serpent.

The red-haired man drew in breath with a sharper hiss. "Just for the life of a blubbering baby-faced milksop, we could have a thousand pounds," he whispered, as if the oaks had ears. "Half for you, half for me. Come on, lass, show me where he hides, and we'll both be rich."

"Go suck eggs," Rowan told him, her voice as hard as her *aelfin* arrowhead.

"Curse you!" The man stepped toward her, threatening, raising his sword higher. "Tell me," he demanded, his voice a growl as menacing as Tykell's. "Speak now, or I'll beat it out of you: Where is he?"

Everything inside Lionel had gone as blank as snow. He could not move either to attack or to flee. But beside him Etty set her jaw, picked up a sizable stone, and flung it as hard as she could. Hurled at short range, it struck true. The forester dropped his weapon and fell forward. Ettarde stepped out of the ivy, picked up another rock, and conked him for good measure. The forester lay still.

Lionel took a breath and found that he could move

again. Stiffly he stood, then walked forward to stand by Etty. Rowan lowered her bow and stepped down from her rocky perch. The three of them looked down at the forester.

"Toads have mercy." Rowan sounded dazed.

"Now what?" asked Ettarde, her voice shaky. "Rowan, he—he knows too much. We have to—"

"No." The word jumped out of Rowan before Etty could finish.

Ettarde turned to her. "But we *have* to! What if—"

"Etty, you know I can't kill a man in cold blood!"

"Not in hot blood either," Lionel grumbled. Something inside him had gone wolf still again. He bent and heaved the limp forester onto his shoulder. Straightening, he said, "I'll take him to Fountain Dale and leave him there. Someone will find him."

Etty looked up at him, her fair eyes wide with fear and surprise. "Lionel . . ."

"Rowan's right," he told her. "Anyway, it doesn't matter."

This was true. He could no longer deny that he was the reason Rowan was in danger. He knew now what he had to do.

You are Lionel of the Rowan Band. . . .
That night an icy wind took the clouds away, and

the stars shone so crisp and near that they seemed to hang in the branches of the oaks and rowans. Lionel lay awake with his back all too thinly blanketed against the stones of the rowan hollow and his eyes wide open, gazing straight up at stars like glittering thistledown.

When he felt sure the others were sleeping, he sat up silently, with none of his usual moaning and groaning. Flanking the embers of a fire lay Rowan and Etty, asleep, bundled in their mantles. Like Lionel, unless they needed to shelter from rain, they kept to the rowan hollow. Rook preferred his cave. Tykell sometimes lay by Rowan, keeping watch as he pressed his furry body against her, but tonight he was off hunting or roaming the night, and Lionel was glad. With the wolf-dog gone, it would be easier for him to slip away.

As quietly as he could, he stood. Etty did not move, and Rowan only sighed, turned her head, then settled into sleep, with starlight on her like a blessing. For a long moment Lionel stood looking at her, memorizing her face, its strong, almost boyish lines gentled by the night. Daughter of Robin Hood, granddaughter of the aelfe themselves, she was like no one else he had ever known.

Would he ever see her again?

He pressed his lips together, fumbled under the collar of his jerkin, and found the thong on which he wore his strand of the silver band, the many-in-one gimmal ring that had belonged to Rowan's mother, Celandine, the half-aelfin seeress. Lionel pulled the thong over his head, then held the silver circle, warm from his body heat, in the palm of his hand. Stepping softly, softly, he stooped over Rowan and laid the silver ring by her head—it settled on the stone with a whisper of sound like the ringing of bluebells, like an omen. When Rowan awoke in the morning and saw it there, she would know that he was gone for good.

Lionel looked a moment longer at Rowan. He wanted to place over her the blanket he was leaving behind, but he could not risk awakening her. He blinked and turned away.

Swallowing hard, he bent and picked up the blue onion-shaped bag in which he carried his harp, a spare jerkin, and—and at this point not much else. With greatest care to be silent, he slipped over the stone wall of the hollow, out of the rowan grove, and away, moving more like an outlaw than he ever had in his life. He did not know where he was going. It didn't matter. All that mattered was to draw the chase away from her and direct it where it belonged: to his own stupid, hulking body.

Probably he would be killed. So be it.

Seven

In a forest hollow he knew well, a good league north of the rowan grove, Lionel crouched by a dead tree, holding his harp in both hands and memorizing the shape of its warm wood burnished by his touch, the way its curves gleamed like old gold in the morning light. Gazing upon it as he had gazed upon Rowan's face. Wondering whether he would ever see it again.

Then with a sigh he wrapped it in his mantle, setting his teeth as the harp disappeared in fold upon fold of cloth. When he had swaddled it well, he placed it in his pack and tied the strings.

Under the white roots of the dead tree, a rocky cavity yawned where once a spring had run—dried up now, like his music. Likely it would never well forth again.

Lionel's throat tightened as he thrust his pack far

back into the shadows beneath stone. But then his jaw in turn tightened, and he stood, turned his back, and strode away. No use looking back. He had a plan to carry out.

"By my troth," Lionel murmured, staring down the Nottingham Way.

Sitting in the middle of that grassy forest track, resting and trying to warm himself in the pale wintry sunshine, he blessed his long legs for bringing him this far in a single night. He'd left Rowan well behind, hidden his harp, and now he heard hoofbeats approaching from beyond the curve in the Way. It couldn't be going better. The rider was coming into view—

"By my *very* troth."

Lionel brightened at the sight of a two-headed monster he remembered well. A black steed with a rider armored in black horsehide. Guy of Gisborn.

Lionel stretched, then rose to stand at the wayside, wishing he wore his foppish finery instead of his shabby brown jerkin and leggings. But the long, girlish, fawn-colored hair curling down around his shoulders should mark him well enough. That, and his big, blinking, baby-blue eyes. Despite the hammering of his heart, he settled one elbow against a young ash tree, insolently lounging.

At a trot the black charger neared him. Seeing how Gisborn spurred the horse and curbed it at the same time, Lionel clenched his teeth. He tried a look at Gisborn's thin-lipped face but could not see the man's eyes in the shadow of the horsehead Gisborn wore by way of visor. Just as well. Those eyes were bound to be cruel.

Riding almost abreast of him, Gisborn hadn't noticed him yet. Probably took him for a tree. With his best smirking cheer Lionel hailed him. "Hallo there."

Gisborn jerked the reins so hard, the horse lifted onto its hind legs. "You!" he shouted, his manly roar cracking with surprise. "Who—"

"Lionel, son of Lionclaw," Lionel told him quite loudly and clearly; he wanted no doubt about this. "At your service, Horsehead," he added, but instead of bending in a courtly bow, he gave Gisborn a finger-in-the-nose salute. Then he ducked into the woods and ran.

"Halt! Outlaw!" shouted Gisborn. Lionel heard the black steed's hooves thundering after him, branches rattling and snapping as Gisborn crashed through them.

Good. He veered northward, away from the rowan grove, and ran like—like an outlaw. Brushing through bracken, bursting through fir and holly, Lionel leapt rocks and roots without breaking stride, his heart beating like eagle wings. Lunging through a thick stand of hemlock, he heard the clattering hooves slow behind him, and he knew—as a rush of glee sent him springing over the trunk of a fallen tree—he knew he could get away. Gisborn's black charger was not made to bound like a deer through the woods, and Gisborn was likely to get himself decapitated by a tree limb if he rode too fast. Far behind him Lionel heard Gisborn cursing. In a few minutes he would lose the bounty hunter entirely, and then Gisborn could go sulking back to Nottingham and tell the Sheriff and the king's foresters and all the other bounty hunters that Lionclaw's son was last seen heading north, nowhere near a certain rowan grove. *Good. Damn them all, let them keep far away from her.* Lionel lunged through a thicket of whortleberry—

And choked back a scream as he dug in his heels and grabbed a tree trunk to keep from hurtling into a river. At his feet the steep bank fell away, and the water that roiled below him looked drowning deep and stormy cold.

Lionel felt cold too. His heart was a hunted stag now, terrified, trying to bound out of him, yet he couldn't seem to breathe, couldn't seem to get his big feet untangled and moving. His hair caught in a whitethorn bush. He lost precious moments before he managed to jerk it free without ripping his scalp off. Running as fast as he could—not nearly fast enough— he trotted along the riverbank, his chest tight, trying to think.

Hoofbeats sounded behind him, far too close. "You're trapped, outlaw!" Gisborn shouted, jeering.

"Mother of mercy," Lionel whispered, groaning, for ahead he saw the land fall away anew. Some stream joined the river there. He could hardly have been more well and truly trapped. A few strides would take him right to the tip of the arrowhead of land at the confluence.

What to do? Double back? But that would put him even nearer to Gisborn. Try to cross the river? If he didn't drown, he'd most likely die of pneumonia afterward. If he could get across the stream somehow and keep running . . . Lady have mercy, he was tired, but . . . maybe. He could hear the horse galloping the same scant distance behind him, its legs no longer than his—

Just as he thought it, Lionel felt his toes catch on something, a rock or a root perhaps. Four hooves instead of two big stupid feet, he realized as he fell, gave the horse an advantage.

He fell flat on his gut, heard Gisborn's yell of triumph, heard the black hooves bearing down. In a moment he would feel the bounty hunter's sword slice into him—

Lionel clenched his eyes shut, let out a heartfelt whimper, then gasped for breath and heaved with his arms and legs, rolling sideward.

There was a sickening drop, then an equally sickening shock as he hit the water. Yes, it was cold. Very. And swift.

On the other hand, just as he went under, Lionel heard Gisborn scream a truly gratifying curse upon his head.

Then the icy water did the running, and within a few moments Lionel had no strength left to force his head to the surface. He caught one breath of air, then a breath of water, which hurt atrociously, and then he no longer knew which way was up as the river tumbled him along. How very strange to feel small, to be tossed around—and then he smashed against something stony, and everything went black.

"Wuff."

Lionel groaned, keeping his eyes closed—they felt frozen shut. *If I can feel this cold and still be alive, I'd rather be dead.* Something was breathing in his face, warm breath that stank like rotten meat. It just made the rest of him feel more frozen. Very well, if there was a wolf standing over him, it could just go ahead and eat him.

Blast. It was licking his face.

Groaning anew, Lionel turned his head away. But moving was a mistake. It started him coughing, and coughing took over. Spasms of coughing shook him worse than the river, lifted him off the ground, then brought him to his knees and tried to turn him inside out. On his hands and knees in icy mud, Lionel coughed until stuff ran out of his eyes and mouth and nose, until his aching ribs couldn't take any more. Still heaving weakly, he gasped for breath.

"Wuff." Meat Breath licked his ear.

Lionel cleared one eye with his fist and peered. Damn, it was Tykell, which meant that Rowan was not far away, which meant that everything had gone wrong. "Tykell," Lionel begged, "go away!"

"Lionel," said a low voice he had heard a few times before. A husky voice. Perhaps a bit huskier than usual.

Lionel reared to his knees, still trying to catch his breath and equally trying to catch hold of his situation. Freezing mud. Icy gray water flowing close by. Gray clouds scudding in a cold sky, gray oaks swaying in a cold wind. Sound of his own teeth chattering. Wild boy, standing there.

"R-R-Rook?"

Half naked as always, panting, Rook looked wet. At first Lionel thought that somehow Rook must have taken a dunking in the river too. Then he realized that the wild boy was wet with sweat.

"Get up," Rook said.

"C-can't." Lionel could barely speak, which was annoying; there was a great deal he wanted to say to Rook. *Good gracious, my dear fellow, have mercy, I'm half dead from that dreadful river; did you see? Did Tykell pull me out? What are you doing here?* He wanted to tell Rook to wrap him warmly, give him food, then go away, but he could only gasp out, "Need—fire—"

Rook shook his head. "Get up, hurry," he said, and yes, his gruff voice was grainy with some emotion Lionel had not heard in him before. "Rowan's caught. Man trap."

Feeling returned gradually, hurtfully, to Lionel's feet as he ran after Rook. Every stride was torture, but his heart hurt worse.

Rowan . . . How badly hurt? How did it happen?

Rook had told him nothing except that they needed the strength of his arms to spring the trap and release Rowan. Rook and Etty had not been able to manage it.

She's still lying there, hurting. . . .

Lionel stumbled, almost fell, caught himself, and surged onward after Rook. Run, run, life was made of running. He asked Rook none of the questions running through his mind. Talk would have been a waste of breath.

Am I strong enough? Will I be able to bend back the jaws? . . .

It hurt to think about. Lionel focused on getting past the ground in front of him. Rock, root, tangle of ivy, yank his long hair loose from holly, keep running. Rotting log, fallen branch, *Don't trip, hurry, jump, don't fall, run faster.* Dead leaves, mushrooms, bracken, thorn thicket, *Run through.* Damn hair catching, tear it loose. Pain, who cared. Legs hurt, chest hurt, heart hurt worse. *It's my fault this happened.* Despite pain, despite numbing weariness, Lionel ran at Rook's heels, pushing the pace.

Quite suddenly Rook fell and lay gasping. Running past him, *Can't stop,* Lionel barked, "Get up!"

Rook lifted his head just enough to shake it. Lifted one hand just enough to point. Lionel ran on, following Tykell now.

Faster! I can keep up with you.

Through blackthorn, oak, beech, elm groves, fronds of mistletoe and dangling grapevine . . . Tykell slowed and whined.

"Go on!" Lionel urged in a whisper. But Tykell growled deep in his chest, bristling, yet held his ears at a slant, uncertain. Lionel halted and grabbed a tree trunk for support. *Which way? Where is Rowan?* He wanted to scream—

The loudest sound in the forest was his own panting, every breath a gasp. He gulped air, then managed to hold it for just a moment.

There. He could hear. Straight ahead, someone crying.

He lurched forward. Tykell followed, whining.

She didn't hear him coming, or perhaps she didn't care. Etty, standing amid golden leaves and silver tree trunks in the fairest beech grove he had ever seen, crying hard and ramming fiercely at the leaf-strewn ground with the butt of a large branch. Then a clang of steel that made Lionel's pounding heart stop for a moment before it tried to burst his chest open. Massive toothed jaws bit deep into the branch now.

He walked forward, staring. Ettarde stared back at him with eyes like pools of gray-green water. "They came on horses and took her," she said.

Lionel looked at the massive trap, then at her, uncomprehending.

"They wore helms and chain mail," Ettarde said. "Arrows wouldn't have— All I could do was hide and watch."

No. None of this could possibly be happening.

"Two men," Etty said. "Two strong men, to spring that trap, then reset it."

Lionel managed to get his mouth moving. "Where is Rowan?" he whispered.

"I told you, they took her! They slung her like meat behind a saddle—"

"But where? Took her where?"

She pointed to the northwest. "All I could do was hide!" she cried, as if that were worst of all. "Waiting for you."

Lionel nodded, looking off the way she had pointed. Oaks, mistletoe, hemlock, holly, thorn thickets fit to conceal any kind of danger. Tykell stood whining, staring the same direction.

"Come on," Lionel said, and he started walking.

"Come on, where?"

"Follow," he said.

Eight

Slowly, too slowly, casting about for the scent, Tykell led them out of the beech grove and across a rocky hilltop where the wind swept hard between thin trees.

"For the love of the Lady," Lionel whispered between his teeth, pacing after the wolf-dog, "I could crawl faster. Where was he when—when it happened?"

Walking at his side, Etty did not answer. He looked at her, saw dirt and tears smearing her royal face, saw the way she did not look back at him, and felt his heart shrink.

"Trailing me?" he asked.

She did not speak, but her glance accused him.

"It's my fault," he said, less as a question than as a certainty.

Still crying, and probably trying not to, she glared at him and burst out, "Why did you have to run off?"

He did not answer. Could not think of the answer. Could not think why everything he did seemed to hurt someone. Could think only of what had happened to Rowan.

He said, "You came looking for me." And curse his stupidity, he should have known that was what Rowan would do. "You came after me. All of you. Places you don't usually walk. And she—"

"Never mind that now. Where's Rook?"

"Collapsed." And no wonder. Rook had run twice the distance he had, on legs not as long.

"But—but how will he find us?"

"I don't know."

Silence. Lionel heard Etty's sobbing quiet to ragged breathing. He heard her blow her nose on the kerchief she kept tucked in the sleeve of her brown woolen frock. He heard jackdaws barking in the distance. Tykell led them a winding way between rabbit warrens, down a hillside deep in vines.

"Horses couldn't have come here!" Lionel burst out.

"Shhh. Follow Ty."

Both fallow deer and the larger red deer leapt out of the vines and away. Tykell did not so much as glance at them. Holding his plumy tail low and still, he trotted with his head up, sampling the air, across a hollow where acorn caps lay thick on the ground, then up the next hillside.

"He's leading us by her scent in the air," Etty said, doubt in her voice.

Silence.

Tykell wormed a prickly way through a stand of holly, looked back over his thickly furred shoulder to see that they were still with him, then trotted on.

Lionel asked Ettarde the question he had not dared before. "How badly is she hurt?"

"I don't know." Etty's voice shook. "It caught her by both legs. She screamed once, then fainted."

"Blood?"

"When they took her out, yes."

"Did she—did she know—"

"She didn't know. She lay like a dead . . ." Etty's voice trailed away.

At the top of the hill ran a deer trail. Tykell paused, whiffing the wind, then took the narrow path. Lionel followed, barely noticing his own limping, his feet rubbed to bloody blisters as his wet boots dried and stiffened. He felt only the pain in his heart, like a dagger wound in his chest. At some time the chill wind had blown the clouds away, and the sun shone down from a sky as cold and blue as his father's eye. Sunshine lit the plane trees from behind, setting their fluttering leaves ablaze with primrose yellow, Lionel's favorite color—but blue sky, sun glory, shining yellow leaves were all a mockery. How dare the sun shine when Rowan . . .

He could scarcely bear to think it, but he had to say it. "Rowan . . . Rowan might already be dead. They may have killed her by now."

Lagging behind him, Etty whispered, "Don't."

"But why did they not take her head at once?"

"Don't, Lionel! Please!"

Let her live. Please let her live, and my father can have me.

Tykell growled and stiffened to a halt on the deer trail, the hair on the back of his neck ruffled, his head lowered, questing. "What is it?" Etty asked.

Lionel did not care what it was. "Go on." He tried to walk forward, but Tykell sidestepped, blocking his way.

"No, stupid!" Etty grabbed his arm. "It's a pile of leaves."

A pretty drift of fallen leaves, yellow and golden, and Lionel hated every one of them. Blast, there was no time for this. He wrenched a branch from a tree and swept it across the trail. Leaves scattered, and there, like a huge, fanged steel toad, squatted the trap, its massive, jagged jaws yawning. Lionel kicked hard at its frame, and it sprang shut with catapult force, *clang,* like a dungeon door. Lionel thought of those great toothed jaws snapping shut with such deadly force on a human leg . . . on Rowan's legs. . . .

No. There was no time for heartsick thoughts. "Come on," Lionel grumbled.

Tykell led off, but Etty veered into the woods. "Don't use the trail. Walk to one side."

"It'll take too long. Come *on.*" Lionel strode after Tykell, not even looking back to see whether Etty was following.

His long strides crowded Tykell, urging the wolf-dog into a lope. The deer trail climbed the crest of a ridge, encountered a rocky scarp, plunged beneath it, and edged along a steep slope deep in pine needles. Tykell halted again, whiffing the wind and muttering deep in his throat. Necessarily, Lionel halted, and Ettarde trotted up behind him, panting.

"Go!" Lionel urged Tykell.

"No! Listen," Ettarde gasped.

Then Lionel heard it also. From not too far below, at the base of the hill, came the muffled clopping of hooves in forest loam, and men's voices.

". . . duty's to our liege king," one said.

"But Lionclaw's the king's favorite," said the other. "Think of it! A thousand pounds, gold—"

"We don't have him yet."

"No, but we have his precious Rowan."

The wind shifted. The sound of hoofbeats and voices faded. Lionel stood for a moment with the breath knocked out of him, as if he had taken a blow to the chest. Then with a gasp he leapt into a run, down the hillside and after them.

Something struck him hard on the side of the head. He saw a burst of light, then only darkness.

Lionel awoke to find himself lying facedown in pine needles, with a painfully throbbing head. He groaned, planted his hands on the ground, and tried to push himself upright, but he couldn't. There seemed to be a weight on his back holding him down.

"Stay where you are," said the weight, thereby identifying itself as Etty.

Lionel's mouth opened, and pine needles inserted themselves. "What?" he sputtered, spitting them out. Then he sputtered anew as Tykell licked his face.

"Stay," said another voice, husky and deep.

"Rook?"

"Man traps below," said Rook.

"You would have galloped straight into a row of man traps if Rook hadn't stopped you." *Idiot,* said Etty's tone of voice. "If I let you up, will you sit still? Those foresters are pitching camp down below, and we need to make a plan."

Lionel did not answer, but Ettarde seemed to take his silence for consent. He felt her weight lift off him, and he sat up, rubbing his head and blinking at Rook standing before him, leaning on his staff—a walking stick, rather, crude and freshly cut.

"You conked me with that?"

"Threw it."

Lionel inspected the sticky blood on his fingers. Not too much blood. "Am I supposed to thank you?"

"My dear big lad," said Rook, blank-faced, "just rest." Already Etty had collapsed to the ground, and Rook swayed where he stood. He sat down beside her, easing a large canvas pack from his back to the ground, then fumbled with the fastenings, his hands shaking. Lionel sat watching, dazed, as Rook pulled out bread and cheese.

Bread and cheese! Lionel babbled, "Where did you—"

"Stole their supper when they stopped for water."

"But—" Etty sounded as bewildered as if she, also,

had been conked on the head. "Rook, how are you here?"

"They rode past where I lay. I followed."

Trying to eat bread, Lionel found that he could not swallow. He could not look at Rook, either, as he asked, "Did you see her? Did you see Rowan? Is she—"

The wild boy gave him a look that quelled him into silence, then pulled a dagger from his belt and plunged it into a round of hard cheese. He stabbed the cheese again, harder, and again, and seven times more before he took a deep breath and laid the knife on the ground.

Silence.

Rook said, "My father died in a man trap."

Lionel became aware of every sound for a league around, of Etty breathing and wind sighing in the pines and a falcon's flight whistling in the twilight sky and somewhere a mouse screaming as it died in the jaws of a weasel.

Rook glanced up and pointed at the bread Lionel held in his hand. "Eat that. Force it down."

"Can't." Lionel laid down the bread but reached for the dagger Rook had laid on the ground. His long hair had dried into snarls studded with twigs and thorns. Lionel grasped a hank of it with one hand and sawed it off with the dagger.

"Don't," Etty said. "I can comb it out for you."

Lionel shook his head, flung away the tangle of hair, grabbed another and kept cutting. He asked Rook, "Is she still alive?"

"I think so."

"They are keeping her alive? To bait me?"

"Yes."

"But . . . I don't understand. How do they know?"

Gnawing at his own hunk of bread, chewing slowly and struggling to swallow, Rook did not answer.

Her voice wavering, Etty said, "Maybe they heard me cry out her name."

Rook told Lionel, "The forest has ears. You sang of her to Lionclaw, that night."

Lionel felt every muscle go taut. His hand shook with tension as he hacked at his hair. Lock after tangled lock fell to the ground. No fawn-colored curls for him any longer. The shorn hair lay dark with sweat and blood.

When he had only stubble left on his head, Lionel tossed the dagger back to Rook.

"Eat your bread and cheese," Rook told him.

Lionel ate. He knew he needed to, for strength. He did not speak, for there was nothing more to say.

Half naked like the wild boy, his blistered feet wrapped in strips of rag torn from his discarded jerkin, Lionel crept like a stalking wolf toward the yellow glare of the foresters' campfire. Against the twilight sky, oaks loomed like kings darkly crowned with mistletoe, offering Lionel sheltering shadows as he wormed his way through brush with scarcely a rustle. Off to one side an owl hooted; that was Rook. Closer at hand a cricket chirped; that was Etty. Lionel squeaked like a mouse. Let the foresters think that was all he was, a mouse. Many had thought so before.

Off to his other side something growled low. He hoped it was Tykell.

Pausing to quiet his breathing and scout his next few steps, Lionel saw a shadow looming black between him and the campfire. A shadow not quite shaped like a man.

". . . bold as brass," said a barking voice. "Taunting me."

Taking three careful steps forward, Lionel considered that he recognized that voice, not to mention the silhouette of a horse's head where a man's should be.

"If he's not a lion, he's the biggest, boldest fox puppy I've ever seen. Daring me after him."

Crouching behind hemlock boughs within a few paces of the campfire, Lionel saw that he was right: Guy of Gisborn had joined the two foresters.

He didn't care. Where was Rowan?

There. At the horses' feet. Thrown on the ground without even a blanket for comfort. Her face far too pale and still in the firelight.

Within arms' reach of each of the three men.

There could be no hope of rescuing her until something changed.

It was bad luck, the worst of luck, that Gisborn had happened along. Lips tight, fists clenched, Lionel studied the three men. Two burly foresters, their bearded heads bare but still wearing their mail and tabards, hunkered by the fire, where there roasted a fine haunch of the king's venison—the meat they set man traps to protect. If they missed their pouch of bread and cheese, they weren't about to starve. Over them stood Guy of Gisborn, with his horse-skull helm pushed back, gesturing like a swordsman as he held forth.

". . . hunt him down tomorrow," he was saying. "Or find his carcass lying downstream. Either way, he will be mine."

"Nah, Horsehead, you'll be wasting your time," said one of the foresters.

"What do you mean?"

"Forget your cold trail. The hot bait's here." The man grinned. Lionel bit his lip so hard, he tasted blood, and it seemed to him he heard the wind rising, hissing in the oaks, hurling darkness across the moon. Far off in the forest a wolf howled.

No fool, Gisborn looked at the unconscious girl strewn on the ground. "Her?"

"Rowan Hood, forsooth. Your overgrown puppy will be sticking his neck out for her. Not to speak of the old fox. Her father, the song says. Robin Hood."

"Bah." Gisborn raked the foresters and their prisoner with a scornful glance, then shrugged. "Lord Lionclaw's men-at-arms speak of a girl in a song, and you believe it? Anyway, Robin Hood's in Barnesdale Forest, so folk say, and that insolent pup—"

"He'll be ours, I tell you. Because we have *her.*" As if booting a stick farther into the fire, the forester kicked Rowan's sprawling, bloodied leg. Her eyelids fluttered, and she moaned.

Force of fury such as he had never known shot Lionel to his feet. He strode forward, out of the shadows and into the full glare of the firelight, within a few paces of the foresters and Gisborn. "Puppy's here," he said.

Nine

For two strong men who bragged of expecting just this, the foresters looked much taken aback. Mouths gaping, they scrambled to their feet. Yanking his horsehead helm over his face, Gisborn crouched and reached for his sword.

He wanted to fight? Fine. With one hand Lionel reached out and seized a young oak tree about the thickness of his wrist. He yanked it up by the roots; his blood was running so fiery hot that he could have yanked up a castle. The tree's root ball annoyed him; he bent the tree over his knee and broke it off, leaving a jagged stump. He twisted off branches by the handful, then lifted his new quarterstaff, both ends of it as spiky and fearsome as Lionclaw's mace. Hefting his weapon, he spread his feet, waiting.

But Gisborn's eyes had gone owlish, shining white

even in the shadow of his helm, and he had not moved. The king's foresters seemed similarly affected. Nobody moved. Nothing moved, not even the wind. The night had gone as still as the clouds veiling the moon.

"Get away from her," Lionel ordered.

Gisborn's wide eyes went narrow again. The two foresters snatched up their swords and inched toward Rowan, as if to seize her—

A wolfish roar froze them. Snarling, Tykell leapt from the shadows to stand over Rowan's unconscious body with his fangs bared, gleaming in the firelight. From the forest to Lionel's left an arrow flew, striking one of the foresters on his mailed shoulder. He yelped with surprise.

"The next one will bury itself to the feathers in your eye," Lionel lied; he knew Etty was not so good a shot. And his heart warmed, for he had expected no help from her. "Get away from her, I say! Cowards, face me!"

How odd, to call someone else a coward.

The foresters glanced at each other and stayed where they were. But Gisborn's black, greedy heart knew no such fear. "The overgrown puppy is mine," he growled. Sword at the ready, crouched for combat, feet shuffling in the loam, he advanced.

As if studying an odd sort of bird, Lionel watched

Gisborn closing on him, a bulky black-leather gargoyle looming in the firelight, hefting his sword with both gloved hands—a heavy, hacking broadsword fit to butcher a man into haunches. "Ooooh, I'm terrified," Lionel taunted. With rage crackling in him like a bonfire, he meant to flatten Gisborn or be chopped up like stew meat. But he told Gisborn with mock solemnity, "The sight of blood makes me sick. I may faint."

Gisborn snarled, "Shut your fool mouth!" and struck.

Lionel met the sword with his makeshift cudgel, feeling the power of the blow shudder up his arms clear to his shoulder blades. With a bellow like a bull, Gisborn struck again, bending the green oakwood like a yew bow.

"Very *good*. You're *strong*," Lionel told him. "Go ahead, more, more!" *A pox on this.* Lionel lunged, his cudgel whistling at Gisborn's head like a giant mace.

Gisborn ducked, letting the spiked weapon pass over his head, and Lionel felt the force of his own blow unbalance him. He saw the foresters circling toward him, swords out. He saw Gisborn coil to strike again and knew he should run. He saw the sword blade flashing toward him—

It's going to hurt my hand!

He saw Rowan lying as still as a corpse.

He roared like a thousand lions, struck the sword aside with his bare hand, and threw the full weight of his body at Gisborn. As he bore the man down, he glimpsed an arrow flying, and a stone, and he heard a forester cry out. A moment later he stood up, with his cudgel in his right hand and his left hand hanging limp, with one foot on Gisborn's chest to hold him down. One forester stood grimacing as he plucked an arrow from his upper arm. The other, blood on his head, stood with sword in hand. Gisborn's sword lay on the ground by his kicking feet. Rook pattered out of the shadows, grabbed it, and positioned himself near Lionel, all without a word.

Lionel felt his battle rage drain away, replaced by a painful clarity that was enhanced by the ache of his hurt hand. Things had become simpler, yet more difficult. The plan had been to rescue Rowan by stealth, if possible—but now Rook stood there hefting a sword too heavy for him. Gisborn lay with the breath knocked out of him, but the two foresters were still very much on their feet. Rook had Gisborn's sword, but Lionel did not want Rook to get hurt. Or Etty. Or Tykell, who had lowered his head to lick Rowan's face, whining.

The foresters stood with swords at the ready, grim-faced. In the silence Lionel heard the flutter of his own heart, the brief scream of a rabbit caught by a fox, and a soft sob from Rowan as she awakened.

"Rook," he said quietly to his comrade, "you and Etty get her, take her away."

Rook shook his head.

"Do it!"

"No. We can best them."

Lionel didn't think so. He had bested Gisborn, but now that he had downed him, now that his rage had passed, he didn't feel as if he had the heart to kill him, and how could he fight anyone else with his foot on Gisborn's chest? Least of all two strong foresters, well armed, inching forward—

Lionel sighed, rolled his eyes, and lowered his monstrous makeshift quarterstaff. "Stop it," he said. Bloodshed would not help Rowan. "Sit down, all of you."

Nobody sat, but everybody stared, including Gisborn, gawking up from the ground.

Lionel said quietly to the foresters, "Let her go, and you can have me."

Gisborn found his breath and began to swear mighty curses upon Lionel. The foresters looked at each other.

"You can have my head right now," Lionel said, and he meant it, for this entire miserable hash was of his making, beginning the night he had thought he would win his father's love with the magic of his singing. Ha. Wretched mistake. What were the blasted foresters hesitating for? Were they perhaps a trifle dense? "My head for her life and liberty," Lionel repeated. "Let my companions take her away, and I won't resist you." He peered at their bearded faces, trying to understand their consternation. "What's the matter? You can kill me any way you want, I'm telling you. Is it my head my dear father wants, or my entire craven carcass?"

One of the men said hoarsely, "Head."

From the far side of the fire came a weak murmur: "Lionel, no . . ."

"Rowan, hush. Save your strength."

The other forester, the one with the arrow wound, blurted plaintively to his companion, "He killed a horse once with a single blow, folk say."

"I did not," Lionel said. "Good gracious mercy, I just knocked it down."

Meanwhile, Gisborn was saying things fit to curdle springwater. Everyone ignored him.

The plaintive forester said, "Suppose we do it . . . but what if Lord Roderick changes his mind?"

"What?"

"Suppose yon oversized poltroon lets us kill him, and Lord Roderick sees his dead face and repents and flies into a rage? Then our heads will be the forfeit. You know there's no wind that blows more fickle than a lord."

Lionel said bleakly, "I don't think he's going to repent."

The other forester took charge. "Listen," he said, "what we do is we take this one prisoner but keep him alive. We keep the girl so he won't resist us, we take them both to—"

"*No!*" Lionel roared, snatching up his oak-tree quarterstaff and brandishing it, rage filling him again like a black fire. "No, let her go. *Now.* Rook, go get her, get her away from here."

Rook did not move. Instead, in his flattest, gruffest tones, he said, "Don't move her. Bring Lord Roderick here."

"*What?*"

"He wants your head—"

"Let him come get it!" Like lightning, Lionel's fury flared into unholy glee. "Yes!" He turned on Guy of Gisborn, lifting his foot from the man's chest, prodding him with his cudgel. "You! Go get him. We'll wait here."

Gisborn scrambled to his feet, grabbing for the dagger he wore at his belt. In a voice like an ice serpent he inquired, "Am I your servant, now, little boy, to do your—"

"GO!" Lifting his gigantic club, Lionel strode toward him.

Gisborn's eyes widened. Without another word he backed away, scrambled onto his horse, and galloped off into the darkness.

Ten

Lionel awoke to a queasy feeling of dread even before he remembered what was wrong. Then he exclaimed, "Rowan!" and sat up, blinking in the half-light of—dawn?

"Shhh," whispered someone—Etty. And yes, it was morning, for Etty huddled by the embers of a campfire, her face weary. Still whispering, she asked, "How is your hand?"

Hand? He glanced down, saw the makeshift bandage wrapping his left hand, spotted with blood. Oh. Yes, from striking Gisborn's sword aside, catching the flat of the blade, mostly. He flexed the fingers. Ow. "It hurts. What does it matter? How's Rowan?"

"Hush. She's resting."

Lionel could see Rowan now, lying with Tykell pressed close beside her and Etty's mantle wrapped around her, between two campfires, theirs and the foresters'. Frost whitened the loam, and only a few hardy birds twittered in the trees. One forester was sleeping, his blanket furred with frost; the other kept guard, stone-faced. Rowan was their prisoner still. But they were allowing her friends to care for her.

A dark half memory made Lionel clutch his own bare, shivering shoulders and mumble, "What happened?"

"You really did faint. After setting her legs."

Lady have mercy, yes, both of her poor legs bloody broken, and because he was the strongest, even with a bruised hand, he was the one who had to pull them straight and hold them that way while Etty and Rook tied the splints around. Dear Lady have mercy, Rowan's pain—he couldn't bear to think of it. Stifling a groan, he closed his eyes.

But he opened them in a moment, stiffened his jaw, lumbered to his feet, and went to kneel by her. "Rowan . . ."

Her lidded eyes did not open; her white face did not answer him. He heard her breathing, rapid and shallow. He touched her hand. It felt ice cold, as if Etty's mantle gave her no warmth at all, it or the horse blankets she lay on—Lionel vaguely remembered threatening them away from the foresters—or Tykell's furry body pressed against her, or the embers of two fires.

"Get that fire going," Lionel told Etty. With his good hand he snatched sticks from the ground and threw them onto the embers. "Is there water in your flask?"

She handed it to him, and he put a finger to the corner of Rowan's mouth and dribbled water in. She did not move.

"Rowan, swallow," he begged.

She did not seem to hear him at all.

"Swallow it! I can't give you more till you swallow." He was afraid of drowning her.

She did not swallow the water. Lionel stood up and turned to Etty. "We should cook her some soup or something. Do we have anything . . ." His words trailed away, for he could not bear to see the look in Etty's eyes, panic and despair that matched his own. Rowan was the healer, not they. Ettarde did not know what to do for Rowan, any more than he did. And Rowan needed more than rescue from them. How to heal the healer?

In the wind the treetops rattled like bones. Above their twiggy fingertips the sun shone dim from a white sky, giving no warmth. Still huddled in the same place, speaking in a bleak tone to the fire, Etty said, "What do we do now?"

On the other side of the fire, roasting fish, Rook glanced up without speaking, gave her a flat look, then shifted his gaze toward Rowan. She lay like white marble. Lionel could not imagine, now, how he had been insane enough to think she could be moved.

Etty said, "Lionel . . ."

"There's nothing we can do but wait, Etty." He tried to keep his voice gentle.

She looked straight at him, and the pain in her eyes made him catch his breath. "Lionel," she said softly, "I'm ashamed."

"Ettarde? But why?"

In the gray light scattering through the branches, her face looked ghostly. She drew her knees to her chest, her hands clenched around them and shaking. She said, "The way I scolded you a few days ago— and now look at what I've done."

"What in the world are you talking about?"

"Me! Useless. I didn't even try to stop them when they came for her. I lost my head, screamed out her name—"

"Oh. Yes—but if you hadn't, they would have killed her then and there."

"I didn't know that. I just panicked, that's all. I ran. I was afraid they would take me too. I ran away."

Out of the corner of his eye Lionel saw Rook look up, then look down again without comment. Numb with cold and worry, he himself could not react much to Etty's admission. He only nodded.

Ettarde said, "If I'd stayed . . . I should have at least tried to hold them off. Maybe I could have shot one in the eye, like you said."

Lionel tightened his lips, got up, and placed more sticks on the fire. To warm Rowan. And Etty.

She said, "And last night—Rook showed himself, but I didn't dare."

"I'm glad you didn't," Lionel said, low. "Shhh." The foresters, blessedly, seemed not to know who she was. But if Guy of Gisborn had seen her, recognized her . . . it didn't bear thinking of.

Eyes on her knees, Etty said, "I'm the coward. I'm the sham. Not you."

"Stop it," Lionel said.

She looked at him.

"Coward, hogwash," Lionel told her. "In your heart you know what you can or can't do. You showed good sense, that's all."

Anyway, this hash was of his cooking, not hers. Blunder after blunder, folly after folly.

She stared up at him. She whispered, "Could you kill someone if you had to?"

"For her . . ." He glanced toward Rowan. "Yes. For anybody else, I don't know." He felt Rook looking at him, met the look, and thought he saw something of understanding in the wild boy's flat, feral eyes.

Lionel whispered, "Rowan? Can you hear me?"

She did not turn toward him or stir. He heard only her restless breathing rasping dry in her throat. That, and the rattling of dead branches overhead.

"Rowan," he tried again, "wake up. Drink some water. Eat a little bit of fish."

It had been three days now. How long could she live this way? He watched her eyelids, so pale they showed snowy blue shadows, for any movement. But there was no moth-wing flutter of awareness. Nothing.

This could not be. Her life was too great a price; why should she pay for his stupidity? His eyes stung. Blinking, he whispered, his voice wavering, "Rowan, please . . . only speak to me, only live, and I don't care what happens to me."

A hard voice said, "Give up, Lionclaw's son."

"She's as good as dead," said the other.

Lionel did not look up. The two foresters might regard him as their prisoner, but they meant nothing to him except that they were the ones who had—had slung Rowan over the back of a horse like a yearling deer, meat for the killing. . . . Kneeling by Rowan with his head bowed, Lionel had to clench his fists and close his eyes to hold back burning rage and scalding tears. Damn them, they should keep silence if they could not understand. They had never known Rowan's gaze as candid as springwater, had never felt the warmth of her smile, had never seen her send a flint-tipped, peacock-feathered arrow skimming into a far target, had never seen her slip through the rowan grove as silently as one of the forest spirits, her kin—

Lionel stiffened bolt upright, and his eyes snapped open. "The aelfe," he whispered.

Eleven

Are you out of your *mind*?" Crouched by the fire, Rook glared up with as much vehemence as Lionel had ever seen in him.

"I don't know how else to summon them," Lionel said.

The bare oaks swayed in a chill wind, the sun hanging like a woolly white ball in their clacking branches. It would be a cold night, and already wolves howled. But no matter. Lionel knew what he had to do.

"Can you *play* your harp?" Etty asked, nodding at his hurt hand.

He flexed it. The movement hurt abominably, but what worried him more was the aching emptiness in his heart where music should have been. There had been no wellspring of music in him since that night— since his father . . .

"Lionel?"

He answered Etty, "I don't know. But I have to try. I *have* to."

Rook did not agree. "You're crazy. You think that if you call spirits—"

"If you'd ever seen the aelfe, Rook, you'd believe." Etty got up, moved around the fire, and stood between them and the foresters as if to shield them. "Lionel, I'll go."

"No. You don't know where I left it." And also, although Lionel did not say it, she could not run as fast as he could to find his harp and bring it back. If Rook would offer to go—but no, the wild boy did not believe. And Lionel could still run faster. "I'm just trying to promise you both I will be back," he said. "Rook, you'll stay with Rowan?"

Rook gave him a fierce look but nodded.

"At least wait until after dark?" Etty asked. "Until one of them is sleeping?"

"No." Lionel could not wait another minute. He turned toward the foresters' campfire, scanning Rowan—yes, she was still breathing, but her pallor harrowed his heart. Careful to keep his hands slack and his face without expression, he strode toward the foresters.

Huddled by their fire with mantles and blankets

wrapped around their shoulders, they stared without moving as Lionel approached. "*Now* what?" barked the bolder one.

Lionel forced himself to smile as he ambled around the fire to stand close behind them. "A word in your ears, my good fellows." In a friendly, fawning way he bent over them, placing his hands lightly on their shoulders.

It was as if he had put salt on slugs. They shrugged irritably. "Bah! Hands off!"

Fine. He raised his hands, seized their heads, and cracked them together as hard as he could.

But they did not conk out, blast them, only howled, then roared, struggling to reach under their mantles for their weapons as Lionel threw himself on top of both of them. He found himself wrestling with the bolder one amid a great tangle of blankets as the other one reeled to his feet. Lionel glimpsed him swaying overhead, sword raised, and thought with mild regret, *Oh no, I'm dead*—but then there was a whack of wood on the man's skull, a yelp, and the sword fell to the frozen ground with a clang. "Lovely!" Lionel called to Rook as Rook hefted a makeshift cudgel of firewood.

"Get up," Rook growled, lunging at the disarmed forester with his club again.

Lionel grabbed the dropped sword, thrashed against

blankets, and blundered to his feet, wheeling to face the more dangerous forester, expecting to meet him sword to sword—but Ettarde had gotten there ahead of him with her weapon of choice, the hefty stone. The man lay tangled in his own mantle and knocked cold.

"My compliments," Lionel told Etty, turning on the remaining forester with upraised sword. Seeing him coming, the man made a puppyish noise and froze, empty hands lifted. Lionel saw that Rook's cudgel had raised a bloody welt on his face. A moment later the man folded to the ground.

"Tie him up," Lionel told Rook. "Tie them both up. Take their weapons."

Rook gave him a look that said instructions were not necessary. "*Go* if you're going."

"Wait." Etty pressed her water flask into his hands, and a packet wrapped in dock leaves.

"What's this?"

"Food."

"No. You—"

"We have enough. *Go.*"

Lionel went. "Take their blankets!" he called over his shoulder as he sprang into a run. "Keep Rowan warm!"

For the tenth time Lionel fell. He had caught his foot on something—a stick, a root, it was impossible to say in the night. He hurtled headfirst into darkness, hands flung out, feeling thorns rake him. Within a breath he got up and ran on, barely aware of something hot and sticky on his skin—blood. It didn't matter. Nothing mattered except saving Rowan, if indeed she was still alive. . . . *No. Don't think it. Think of nothing.* Except running, run, run, keep running, peering into the tricky shadows. Taking the straightest way through the forest, following no trail, Lionel did not let himself think of getting lost either, or of man traps, or of failing to find the harp where he had left it. He thought only *Run,* run, around the fallen oak, down the ravine and through the stream, up the other side. Eyes on the next stride, run, through willow hollow, redberry rift, rocks, and bracken, hearing nothing except his own footfalls, his own hard breathing, his own pulse roaring in his ears, his own thinking. *Run, run,* Rowan, Rowan, Rowan, Rowan, her name like a heartbeat in his mind.

Run, run through blackthorn thicket and ivy tangle, through hornbeam, and hemlock, until he fell again, this time because he could run no more. When he could move, he heaved himself up to rest his back against a stump and forced himself to eat cold fish and stale bread from the packet Etty had given him. When he had eaten somewhat and sipped water, he tottered up and ran on.

Run, wet leaves slipping underfoot, run, eyes stinging with sweat, jump the grapevine snaking from shadows no longer black. Lionel flicked a glance toward the sky, saw dark limbs looming against dove-gray dawn. He had run through the night, and yes, yes, running, he knew this stretch of forest. He could not have said how, but he recognized these rocky, wooded hillsides the way he might recognize the face of a friend. Just beyond the next elbow of land lay the Nottingham Way.

Run. One foot in front of the other. Run.

On legs that felt like wood Lionel staggered onto the grassy track, turned southward, and ran more strongly. Dawn bloomed like a poppy, warming the sky, and it was not far now to where he had left his harp. Just around the curve—

Lionel lurched to a halt and stood gasping and staring at what he saw on the track in front of him: campfires. Men hunkered by the campfires. Men rolling their blankets, men eating a too-early breakfast, men saddling horses, men yawning.

Men who wore the livery of Lord Roderick Lionclaw.

And by the largest fire, in the very lap of the plane-tree grove where Lionel's harp lay hidden, sat a burly, bearded man who made him remember all the cowardly instincts his poor weary body had ever professed.

Lord Roderick Lionclaw looked up, and a black cavity appeared in his beard as his mouth dropped open.

Lionel actually felt his buttocks tighten as if he might be whipped. He felt his throat tighten to whimper. Without consulting him, his body flinched and stepped back, wanting to run, run away—

Rowan.

There was no time for standing and dithering. Lionel set his jaw and leapt forward, running, running, charging into the muddle of men in his way. "Excuse me," he murmured as he shouldered an opening between two soldiers, knocked over an unlucky man who got in his way, then ran on. "Sorry," as he swatted aside a man-at-arms who had the presence of mind to grab at him. "Sorry, no time to chat," as he flattened a hulking man in smallclothes who seemed determined to whack him with a sword. Only when he heard the fellow swear at him did Lionel recognize Guy of Gisborn without his horsehide armor.

Then, directly in front of him, Lionel saw a rampaging lion baring its golden fangs on a tunic stretched tight over a mighty chest, over glinting chain mail. He saw the gleam of morning sunlight on a drawn sword. He saw a jutting, brassy beard. He saw a man like a monolith blocking his way.

As strong and stony as a fortress, great shouldered, spraddle legged, weapon raised to strike, there stood Lord Roderick Lionclaw.

Father.

For a moment Lionel's heart turned over.

But within a heartbeat some force even stronger than stone took hold in him. Father? Just another obstacle. Nothing mattered except running to get his harp. Even though his heart had stopped for a moment, his legs had not. He veered only slightly, trying to brush past—

"Stand, sirrah!" His father slashed at him.

Lionel jerked back from the blow just in time. Forced to halt, he peered at the savage, incomprehensible golden annoyance blocking his path. "I have to get my harp," he explained.

"How dare you speak—"

"Now," Lionel added, lunging forward. "Out of my way, please."

Lionclaw did not obey. "Seize him!" Lionclaw bellowed as Lionel charged, hurtling forward like a wild boar, running down anything before him, barely noticing the men who clutched at him before he tore away. He batted his father's sword aside with one hand as he rammed into him. It was like hitting a stone wall. Lionclaw did not topple, but he staggered, and Lionel swept past him, running into the plane-tree grove for his harp.

From the Nottingham Way just behind him came shouted commands. Of course they would pursue him just as soon as they could sort themselves out and sling on their gear. But that knowledge was not what made Lionel's heart pound. It was the thought of holding his harp once again that made his heart drum harder than his running feet.

There.

Nestled under the roots of a dead tree as stark and white as a skeleton, there was the rocky cavity where once a wellspring had run. It had long ago gone dry, but for some reason Lionel's heart felt springwater bubbling full and overflowing with intimations of music. Nothing, not a hurt hand, not the price on his head, not even his father could take this away from him ever again. Plunging to his knees, Lionel reached in, fingers seeking—yes. Lady be thanked, the pouch that protected his harp was still there. He snatched it up, sprang to his feet, and ran on, veering westward now, heading toward where Rowan lay.

Keep running.

Ribs aching, lungs on fire, throat parched, lips cracking, legs like water.

Run. Run. Rowan, Rowan, Rowan, Rowan . . .

Twelve

W uff."

Tykell? Yes, licking his nose hard enough to polish the hair out of his nostrils, curse it. Lionel groaned and turned his face away. Couldn't think where he was or why he was lying on the ground. Dunked in a river . . . no, that was a different time. He knew he would never take his harp into a river, and he felt its familiar ivy-carved curve in his hand, sensed it as if it were a part of him, not like the hard thing poking into his mouth. Who was trying to force something between his teeth? And what was it? Lionel clenched his teeth and tried to pull his head away, but a fiery liquid trickled down his throat—

Lionel choked, gasped, sputtered, and his eyes snapped open. With a surge of new strength he jolted upright, staring around him. Twilight. Fading sky, oaks burred with mistletoe, yellow glow between the charcoal-dark tree trunks—campfires, two of them. Closer at hand, a skinny, crouching form haloed by shaggy hair—Rook.

I made it back, Lionel realized. The last he remembered, he had been still running, staggering, utterly at the end of his strength, only one thought keeping him going—

Lionel gasped, panicked, and lurched to his feet. "Rowan!"

"Still alive. Barely." Rook stood and led the way toward the campfires.

Following, stumbling along at a fair to middling walk, Lionel saw a bottle glinting in the wild boy's hand. "Brandy?" he murmured, still bewildered.

Rook nodded. "Foresters had it." He sounded curt.

"And they didn't offer—"

Rook cut him off. "She couldn't swallow it anyway. Come on."

Rowan. Run, run . . . Lionel broke into a ragged trot between the oaks, dodged a dangling bough, shouldered through the saplings, and burst into camp. The two foresters sat on the ground, bound hand and foot. Bolting past them, past Etty as she looked up at him with a gasp, Lionel folded to his knees beside Rowan.

Lady have mercy.

Swaddled in mantles and blankets, she looked as small as a child, no, a changeling, a lifeless white stick child carved out of buttonwood. So still. Lionel had to reach out with a shaking hand and feel her throat to sense the flutter of pulse and breath deep beneath her cold, pale skin.

His throat tightened, but he could not whimper. His chest heaved, but he could not weep. This was a matter too grave for weeping. Rowan lay a hair's breadth away from death.

Campfire glow felt cold to Lionel. Tykell huddled close by his side, whining, but the wolf-dog's furred body felt cold to him. The only warm thing in the world now for Lionel was the curve of his harp in his hand.

In his good hand. But the other one—

Lionel flexed his left hand, dimly feeling how it ached, blinking as he noticed its makeshift bandage crusted with dried blood—why so much blood? Oh. From parrying his father's sword. He had to learn to stop doing that, batting at swords with his hand. Dear Lady of mercy, how could he play his harp now? His fingers stuck out of the bandage as stiff as cold sausages.

And could he sing? Damn the stupidity of his life, yes, his music was back, he could feel it, he had never wanted so badly to sing, the bittersweet wellspring of his heart full to overflowing—but he had run too far, he felt barely strong enough to balance himself upright, his arms and shoulders trembling, his throat raw from panting, his voice as weak as a baby bird's. Summon the aelfe to heal Rowan? What a fool he had been to think it. He might summon crows, perhaps, to laugh at him.

The realization cut through him like a spearhead. He wanted to scream, to weep.

Instead, he cradled the harp in his lap. He stroked the strings with his cold, stiff hands and doggedly set about tuning them. Curse and blast it all, he would still sing for Rowan. Heavenly angels take her, Lionel thought.

Oh, Rowan . . .

Just to give Rowan the blessing of music for goodbye, Lionel tuned the strings to sing in angel harmony, strummed his harp, lifted his head, and closed his eyes. With no thought except to ease her passing, he sang.

> *"Alas, my love, you do me wrong*
> *To cast me off discourteously,*

For I have loved you so long
Delighting in your company. . . ."

His voice battled its way, hoarse, out of his swollen throat and cracking mouth. That harrowed, bleeding voice—it barely seemed like his own. He had never sung so wounded. Every word, every note, fought its way like a warrior out of his aching chest, and Rowan was the chieftain to whom they gave their fealty; they lifted their weary, shining swords for her.

Lionel sang of heroes: Robin Hood, Bran the Blessed, King Arthur. He sang of the Knights of the Round Table: Gawain, Tristan, the brothers Balin and Balan. He sang of King Arthur in battle, and he seemed to hear men's shouts—no, screams, warriors screaming—but the cries quickly faded away. He sang of Robin Hood again, and of True Thomas journeying to faery, and of Percival and Galahad questing for the Grail. As he played his harp and sang, the ringing of the strings strengthened him, a princess brought him water to drink, fire glow slowly warmed him, and he sang like a river. As the firelight flickered on his lidded eyes, he seemed to see golden warriors riding, red hawks flying. Like a warrior riding homeward, he felt comforted now, at peace, and he sang of springtime, the lark on the wing, wild roses twining. He sang of the forest, tall oaks and robin and wren, of boars in the thickets and badgers in their dens—and as he sang, Lionel heard other voices joining his, owls singing, and wolves, and Tykell close beside him singing along with the wolf chorus, and—and others.

Singing of the fallow deer, Lionel opened his eyes, and he saw them.

The aelfe.

The deathless dwellers from within the hollow hills. Manifesting only dimly, no more than moon-glow wraiths floating between the mighty trunks of the oaks, still they were the aelfe, and Lionel had to close his eyes again, too heartsore to look long on their glimmering, ageless faces. Noble faces, all of them, whether queenly, or wise, or warrior fierce, or damsel gentle, or lady serene, sad, joyous, innocent, grave—but in every spiritous face Lionel saw Rowan, Rowan, and grief clotted his heart, and he could not bear to look upon them.

He sang for them, now, as well as for her, and he sang of wonders: of the wise salmon feeding forever on hazelnuts in his pool at the roots of the world tree; of a silver swan piercing her breast to feed her young; of a white stag running, its antlers a kingly crown of pure gold. And he sang of Rowan. Rowan Hood, daughter of Celandine, who was a daughter of the aelfe, Rowan of the brave bow and the healing hand, Rowan, dweller in the rowan wood. He sang at last of the scarlet rowan berries dropping into the pool of Rowan's spring. And when he had sung that, he could sing no more.

His heart swollen so great that it blocked his throat, Lionel bowed his head. The last note echoed away into silence deeper than any well. No owl called now, and no wolf sang; there was not even a whisper of breeze to give voice to the oaks, not even the fluttering of a moth's wing. Laying his harp aside, Lionel drew breath, then lifted his head and opened his eyes.

Blinking, as if looking up at the sun, he faced the moon-glow presence of the aelfe. Some few times before, he had ventured to speak with them, but with his heart so full, he found it hard to look into their grave, shimmering faces. Everything depended on them. If only they would smile . . . But spirits did not smile. Neither did they rage, but facing a raging enemy might have been easier.

Lionel got his dry mouth moving and spoke. "Ageless ones," he faltered, "you once offered me a boon. I had no need then, but—may I beg it of you now?"

None of them stirred, yet they spoke. Their voice came not out of their still faces, but out of the night, the forest, the rocks and the oaks and the moon scudding amid clouds. Soft and deep, that voice told him, "Ask on, harper."

He swallowed, trembling now, and spoke. "Mighty ones, if it is within your power—might Rowan live?"

Even if I die, he thought. Even if they strike me dead for my temerity.

They did not answer, but the night answered, air swirling down from the scudding moonlit sky; that gust of wind made Lionel shiver and tremble. But then the cold wind warmed, and in that moment the forest answered, oaks murmuring, wolves greeting the moon, owl hoot and the chuckle of a fox and a woof from Tykell and someone giving a soft sob of joy that was almost a laugh and among all the other voices, one warm, sober voice saying, "Lionel . . ."

He gasped and turned. Sitting up, supported in Etty's arms, Rowan gifted him with her rarest smile.

Thirteen

I thought you were dead," Rowan whispered.

Lionel blinked and touched her hand. Her fingers felt warm now. Kneeling by her side, his harp forgotten, Lionel could not stop gazing at her. With a faint flush of life in her thin face now, but still very weak, she lay in her blankets, Lionel and Tykell and Rook and Etty all clustered around her.

"I thought you had gone away to die," she tried again to explain, "and I didn't want to live. But then I heard you singing . . ."

Through a blur of relief and tears and weariness, Lionel remembered his manners. Wrenching his gaze away from Rowan, he stood up, walked away from the firelight, and looked for the aelfe. The moon had set, but yes, the forest spirits still shimmered between the trees, their thistledown glow muted by a rosy radiance: dawn.

Lionel addressed them humbly: "From my heart of hearts I thank you, holy ones."

But a puff of wind shook the oaks and set them to creaking as if the forest were laughing. Rippling, the voice of the aelfe said, "It was not we who healed her, foolish mortal."

Lionel stood speechless.

"We have given you nothing, harper. What boon can we grant? Ask."

"I—I have everything I need." This was true. Lionel considered that he had his comrades, his harp, his music—few folk knew such blessing. In that moment, looking up at oaks standing regal, crowned by dawn, Lionel knew that not even the king had ever felt so blessed. Not even Robin Hood, king of outlaws, had such happiness. And certainly not that fellow yonder.

Who was he?

Lionel directed his groggy attention to the man hesitating in the shadows of the massive tree trunks, some beggar perhaps wanting to share the warmth of the fire, a solitary figure looking very small amid the vastness of Sherwood, standing like an undersized, stony fortress—

Lionel peered, blinked in surprise, then smiled. "Blessed spirits," he addressed the aelfe, "might I give my boon to yon lord?"

Across the distance between them, Lord Roderick Lionclaw met his eyes, glowering.

The voice of the aelfe rumbled low, displeased. "Yon lord? Why do you wish to grant him your boon, harper?"

"He is my father."

"But are you his son? He has nothing of your heart; your mother gave you that. Although . . ." The voice of the aelfe softened. "Although it is true that he braves our presence when all his retainers ran away. Perhaps it is from him that you derive your courage, harper."

Courage?

Why did Lord Roderick not raise his wrathful voice to correct the aelfe, to tell them his son was an utter, miserable, sniveling coward? Wondering, Lionel walked toward his father until he stood within a few paces of him, face to his scowling face. "Father?" he asked. "Are you all right?"

Without moving his stony mouth, Lord Lionclaw growled, an earthquake rumble deep in his chest. Metal clashed against metal as he drew his sword.

Lionel sighed. "I am weary of swords, Father."

His father's scowl blackened. Lionclaw raised the sword. The blade shivered in air, scattering silver flakes of light. On the hilt Lionclaw's taut fist shook.

"You want my head?" Lionel inquired. "Would that make you smile? Go ahead. Take it."

He waited, more than half expecting his father to strike. But Lord Roderick only stood like quaking stone and glared.

"Is it my hands you want?" Lionel stretched his hands toward his father, noting with hazy wonder the bruises and bloody scrapes on his own bare arms, the bandage black with blood. "My hands," he told his father, nodding. "Smash them. Then I'll never play my harp again; then you'll be happy."

Again Lionel waited. The upraised sword shook harder. Lionclaw trembled all over.

"Father?"

Lord Roderick's trembling sword sank as if he did not have strength to hold it up. His mouth opened at last, gaping like the beak of a fish gasping for air. "What are you?" he demanded in a hoarse whisper.

"I beg your pardon?"

"What *are* you? Where did you come from? You're no son of mine." His father's voice, almost whimpering, sounded all too much like his own did at times.

"But I *am* your son."

"Then why don't you hate me? You should hate me."

This was not a thought that had ever occurred to Lionel. He considered it with wonder. Hate? When dawn was blooming in the sky and all the morning birds were singing?

"You *want* me to hate you?"

"Yes! When will you ever learn?"

Lionel shook his head, owlish with joy and weariness. He stared at his father. His father stared at him. For the first time Lionel noticed gray hairs in his father's jutting beard, like silver wires curling amid the gold. His father's eyes looked like pebbles underwater. Old and cold.

Lionel appealed, "Won't you come warm yourself at our fire?"

"Bah. You're out of your mind." With dead branches snapping under his heavy tread, with his massive sword still clutched in his hand, its tip almost dragging on the ground, Lord Roderick Lionclaw turned and strode away.

Lionel stared as his father's form dwindled into forest shadow, as the whipcrack of breaking sticks faded.

Silence. Lionel took a deep breath of green-scented air. Somewhere sparrows twittered, and in that small sound he seemed to hear a larger laughter. He turned to look for the aelfe but saw only dawn's silvergold glow lighting the oak grove. The spirits of Sherwood were gone.

But close at hand someone chuckled. Out from behind a cascade of ivy stepped a tall man, his brown mantle thrown back from his clothing of Lincoln green: Robin Hood. "Lady have mercy, Lionel," he said, "how does it come to pass that yon lord hath decamped in such disorder? And what hath sent his followers bawling and fleeing? Men-at-arms running and bleating as far as Barnesdale, forsooth, and a pair of babbling foresters, and more Lionclaw retainers than I can fit in a poke, and Guy of Gisborn in his small-clothes, by my beard!" He passed an amused glance over Lionel. "And here you are looking like a wild man, with blood on your hands and cuts on your shoulders and dirt on your face—have you grown fangs too? My dear little lad, do tell: What has been going on in my forest while my back was turned?"

"You should have asked them for a jerkin," said Rook.

Sitting close to the campfire, wearing Robin Hood's mantle over his bare shoulders and soaking his bare sore feet in a basin of warm water, Lionel answered Rook only by wrinkling his nose. The sun shone down warm and golden through the oaks, a haunch of venison roasted over the fire, Rowan lay peacefully sleeping with her father sitting by her side, and all the others could talk of, once they had told Robin all about it, was what boon Lionel should have begged of the aelfe.

"No," Ettarde said, "you should have asked them to keep scaring the foresters and Gisborn and all the rest of them out of the forest till eternity."

Feeling as warm and sleepy as a cottage cat, Lionel yawned and blinked at her. "The foresters broke loose?"

"I cut them loose." Ettarde looked up from the hazelnuts she was shelling in her lap with a sheepish smile. "I couldn't bear to hear them screaming when the aelfe came."

This made perfect sense to Lionel. He nodded, yawned again, lifted his feet out of their basin, and lay back on the ground, staring up through bare shining oak boughs at a hawk circling in an azure sky.

"Want a blanket?" Etty asked.

"No, I'm fine."

"Fine, my eye. You're lank as a wolf. You haven't been eating."

"I'll make up for it."

Rook said, "You should have asked them for roast suckling pork."

"Or a brace of braised peacock, I suppose." Without

more than a brief pang, Lionel remembered feasts at his father's lordly court. Sweetmeats, plum pudding, and marzipan—but really, who cared?

Etty cared, perhaps. Abruptly, as if she had heard his thoughts, she said, "You should have asked to be no longer an outlaw. Lionel, your father—do you think he'll take the price off your head now?"

"I have no idea."

Rook said gruffly, "You should have asked them to give your father a heart."

Lionel lifted his head from the ground just enough to ogle at them owlishly. "But my dear young friends," he told them in his best mincing tones, "bless my bones, it really doesn't matter. Truly."

Lying down again, Lionel saw a hazelnut fly over his face, narrowly missing his nose. He smiled. "My dear lady, don't waste them," he told Etty.

"I'm not your dear lady!"

"Nevertheless, my dear—"

Another hazelnut pinged his ear. Lionel grinned, then fell silent, gazing up at sunlit blue through oaks gleaming with mistletoe. It was true, what he had said: Whether his father took the price off his head did not matter. Whether his father changed did not matter. There had been change enough. In him. Anyway, the circling hawk sang a warrior song in the high sky, and a tendril of smoke rose like a dove from the campfire, and the aroma of roasting venison . . . a ballad in praise of the aroma of roasting venison began to form in Lionel's mind. He stretched his long legs and waggled feet the size of pony heads. He sat up. "By my fat, craven body," he asked, "isn't supper ready yet?"